P9-BYJ-579

D.C. Dead

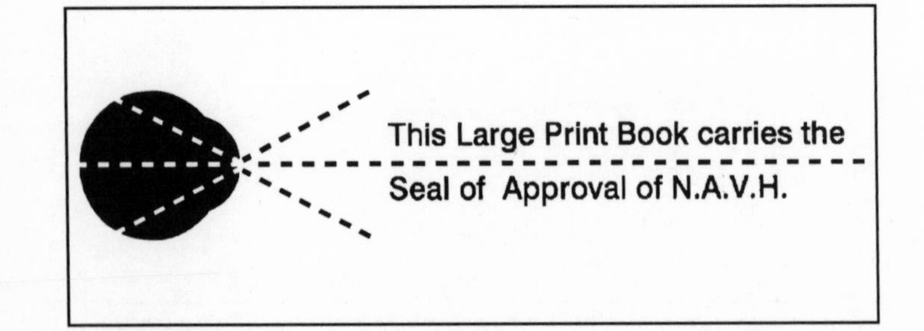

This Large Print Book carries the
Seal of Approval of N.A.V.H.

D.C. Dead

Stuart Woods

THORNDIKE PRESS
A part of Gale, Cengage Learning

WITHDRAWN

Detroit • New York • San Francisco • New Haven, Conn • Waterville, Maine • London

Dunn Public Library

Copyright © 2012 by Stuart Woods.
A Stone Barrington Novel.
Thorndike Press, a part of Gale, Cengage Learning.

ALL RIGHTS RESERVED
This is a work of fiction. Names, characters, places, and incidents either are the product of the author's imagination or are used fictitiously, any resemblance to actual persons, living or dead, businesses, companies, events, locales is entirely coincidental.
While the author has made every effort to provide accurate telephone numbers and Internet addresses at the time of publication, neither the publisher nor the author assumes any responsibility for errors, or for changes that occur after publication. Further, the publisher does not have any control over and does not assume any responsibility for author or third-party websites or their content.
Thorndike Press® Large Print Basic.
The text of this Large Print edition is unabridged.
Other aspects of the book may vary from the original edition.
Set in 16 pt. Plantin.

LIBRARY OF CONGRESS CATALOGING-IN-PUBLICATION DATA

Woods, Stuart.
D.C. Dead / by Stuart Woods. — Large print ed.
p. cm. — (Thorndike Press large print basic)
"A Stone Barrington Novel."
ISBN-13: 978-1-4104-4493-6 (hardcover)
ISBN-10: 1-4104-4493-7 (hardcover)
1. Barrington, Stone (Fictitious character)—Fiction. 2. Private investigators—Fiction. 3. Washington (D.C.)—Fiction. 4. Large type books. I. Title.
PS3573.O642D3 2012
813'.54—dc23 2011041281

Published in 2012 by arrangement with G. P. Putnam's Sons, a member of Penguin Group (USA), Inc.

Printed in the United States of America
1 2 3 4 5 6 7 16 15 14 13 12

This book is for Emmi Storrs

1

Stone Barrington and Dino Bacchetti entered Elaine's on a Sunday evening, and drinks were brought to them immediately.

They took their usual table, and Elaine came over and sat down. "You two are oddly dressed," she said. "For you. What's going on?"

"Oh," Stone said, "we delivered our sons to Yale for their freshman year this afternoon, and we're dressed for humping boxes of their gear up to their apartment."

Elaine nodded. "So the boys are off?"

"They're off," Dino said.

"No wonder you both look so glum," Elaine said.

Stone looked at Dino. "Do I look glum?"

"Yeah," Dino said.

"So do you."

"You're empty nesters now," Elaine chortled. "Never thought I'd see the day."

Stone shook his head. "Nine months ago

I didn't have a son, at least not one I'd ever met. Now I don't have a son again."

Elaine reached over and patted his cheek. "You haven't lost a son," she said, "you've gained a college boy." She got up and continued her rounds of the regulars' tables.

"I guess that's one way to look at it," Stone said. "Do you think he'll ever come home again?"

"Probably not," Dino replied. "You've seen the last of that kid."

"Oh, shut up. You're in the same spot."

"Nah," Dino said, "you're worse off. At least I'm not used to having Ben around the house all the time. He's been at prep school for four years, and then his mother yanked him to her place every chance she got. This afternoon, why didn't you raise the subject of visits home?"

"I thought about it," Stone said, "but I was afraid I wouldn't like the answer. After all, the kid's got the money he was paid for his film, which is more than I had a year ago, so he doesn't need me for anything."

"He just doesn't need you for buying stuff," Dino pointed out. "He still needs a father."

"You really think so?"

"Ben needs me, I'm sure of that. Why wouldn't Peter need you, what with his mother dead and all?"

"He's got Hattie. They're sleeping together, you know."

Dino laughed aloud. "No shit? What were *you* doing your freshman year?"

Stone shrugged. "Fucking my brains out, if I recall correctly."

"Actually, you continued to do that, at least until you and Arrington got married."

Stone managed a smile. "If anything, the activity increased after that."

"I'm getting worried about you, kiddo," Dino said. "You're gonna have to get back in the saddle pretty soon or you're gonna forget how."

"Yeah, I think about that a lot. It's just that . . . well, it's like not being hungry at dinnertime. I just don't have an appetite."

Dino turned and watched as a very pretty brunette in a short skirt came through the door and took a seat at the bar, crossing her long legs. "Doesn't that do anything for you?"

"Sort of," Stone replied. "I mean, I remember what it was like, the way you remember how you roller-skated when you were a kid, but it just isn't all that appealing."

Dino felt for Stone's pulse and looked at his watch. "Your vital signs seem normal."

"That's something, I guess."

"Look who's here," Dino said, nodding toward the door.

Stone turned in time to see a tall redhead in a well-cut pantsuit enter the restaurant. She headed for their table and sat down. "Hello, sailors," she said, leering a little.

Stone leaned over and kissed her. "Hello, Holly. What brings you to town?"

Dino kissed her, too. "Same question here."

"Agency business," Holly Barker replied. She was an assistant deputy director for the CIA. "I hope you guys remember that you're still under contract to us as consultants."

"How could we forget?" Stone asked. "Lance keeps reminding us." Lance Cabot was Holly's boss, deputy director for operations, or DDO.

"Well, fellas, you're about to get the call again."

Stone slumped. "Now what?"

"I can't tell you," Holly replied.

"Can't tell us what?" Dino asked.

"That's what I can't tell you, dummy," she said.

"What kind of deal is this?" Stone asked.

"Here's the deal: you get the daily rate specified in your contract and five hundred per diem."

"For how long?" Dino asked.

"That depends on how good you are," she said.

"Who can live on five hundred a day?" Stone asked.

"Clearly, you've been living too well," Holly replied. "If you stay at a Holiday Inn Express, and eat at McDonald's, you can make money on that. Would you like my office to book you in?"

"Thanks," Stone said. "I'll make my own arrangements."

"He'll make mine, too," Dino said. "He's a regular travel agent."

"As you wish," Holly said.

"Come on, give us a hint."

"Here's the only hint you're going to get," Holly said. "I'll have a car left for you at the Manassas, Virginia, airport. There'll be an envelope locked in the glove compartment containing your credentials."

"Credentials?" Dino asked. "You think we don't know who we are?"

"Sure," Holly said, "but nobody in Washington does. You'll have to prove it, especially at the White House."

"Which White House is that?" Stone asked.

"The *only* one," Holly said. "Find yourselves hotel rooms, then be there at six sharp tomorrow evening, freshly scrubbed and pressed. If you're lucky, you'll get dinner, but don't count on it."

"Is it black tie?" Stone asked.

"You're not *that* important," Holly said. "Just wear one of your nice suits."

"The blue or the pinstripe?" Stone asked.

"Your choice, sweetie. By the way, I'm very sorry for your loss."

"Thank you. I got your very nice letter. I'm afraid I haven't responded to all those yet."

"Don't worry about it."

"How are you and the boyfriend doing?" Dino asked.

"He's running a big trauma center in San Diego," she replied. "He didn't take to the agency life — not enough blood and guts, I guess. It's been a couple of months. It was amicable."

"Let me get you a drink and a menu," Stone said.

"Love to, but can't," she said. "There's a chopper waiting for me at the West Side heliport, and I've got a briefcase full of work to keep me awake on the flight home." She stood up, and both men stood up with her.

"See you tomorrow evening," she said, then walked briskly out.

They sat down again.

"Why did you ask her about the boyfriend?" Stone asked.

"Because I knew you wouldn't," Dino replied.

2

Stone packed a bag the following morning, then, on second thought, packed a second bag. The last time he had consulted for the CIA, he, Holly, and Dino had spent a couple of weeks on a tropical isle, pursuing a federal fugitive named Teddy Fay, who gave them the slip. Who knew how long this one would take or where they would end up?

He took the elevator down to the garage and put his bags in the car, then he went to his office and wondered what to put in his briefcase.

Joan Robertson, his secretary, appeared in the doorway. "You off to someplace?"

"To Washington — for a few days, I think."

"Could be longer?"

"It's one of those things for Lance Cabot and Holly Barker. Who knows?"

"You'd better take your passport," she said, opening his safe and tossing him the document.

"I'd take my vaccinations, if I knew which ones to take," he replied.

"You don't look very happy about this," Joan said, pouring him a cup of coffee.

"I'm not unhappy about it," Stone replied. "If I'm unhappy at all, it's about Peter's being off at Yale."

"How did yesterday go?"

Stone shrugged. "Bittersweet. I'm happy for Peter, getting what he wants, but I miss him already."

"So do I," Joan said. "It was a nice change from it being just you all the time."

"You'll have Allison to talk to," Stone said, referring to the Woodman & Weld associate who had been assigned to his office, "and that means you'll have Herbie Fisher dropping by at every opportunity just because Allison is here."

"I hear on the secretarial grapevine that Herbie is already making his mark at the firm," Joan said, "working long hours, being smart. He's got the other associates coming to him for answers."

"Who knew that Herbie would turn out so well?" Stone said. "I personally thought he'd be dead or in prison by now."

"Better haircuts and suits seemed to improve him," Joan said, "and the lottery win didn't hurt."

"I hope he's still got some of it," Stone said.

The bell rang, and Joan went to let Dino in. She took his bags to the garage.

"Coffee before we blast off?" Stone asked.

"It couldn't hurt," Dino said, accepting a cup. "Has Holly called and told you what this is all about?"

Stone sat down and sipped his coffee. "Nope. I'm as much in the dark as you are."

"That used to be kind of exciting," Dino said, "not knowing what's going to happen."

"You're depressed," Stone said.

"I am?" Dino said, looking surprised.

"About Ben going away to college."

"Oh, that. Yeah. You too."

"Yeah, me too."

"I have an idea," Dino said. "Let's go to Washington and find out what the hell this is all about. It might improve our dispositions."

"Good idea," Stone said, putting his coat on. "Let's get out of here."

They were at Teterboro Airport in half an hour, and it took Stone another forty-five minutes to do a preflight inspection of his Citation Mustang, get a clearance to Manassas, and taxi to the runway. Shortly, they were cleared for takeoff. Stone shoved the throttles all the way forward, waited for ninety knots, then rotated. The little jet roared off the runway like a big bird. Stone contacted New York Departure, got a vector and a new altitude, and they were off.

Another three-quarters of an hour and they were settling onto the runway at Manassas. A lineman directed them to a parking spot, and someone drove a black SUV over to the airplane and parked it near the door.

"That must be our car," Dino said.

"Who would give us a black SUV but the CIA?" Stone asked.

The lineman took their bags from the forward luggage compartment and stowed them in the rear of the vehicle, then Stone registered with the FBO (Fixed Base Operator) and gave them a credit card for refueling.

"I'll drive," Dino said. "I know the city better than you."

"Nevertheless, I hope there's a map in the car," Stone said.

He got into the passenger seat, and Dino got behind the wheel. "I'm going to need the car key to open the glove box," Stone said.

Dino handed him the keys, and Stone

examined them carefully. There were just two: an ordinary car key and another that looked like something off the space shuttle. He inserted that key into the large, non-standard lock on the glove box and opened it. Inside he found two holstered SIG Sauer P239 9mm pistols with an extra magazine for each, and a box of cartridges.

"Why do we need to be armed to go to the White House?" Stone said. "They'll just take them away from us as soon as we get there."

"Just leave them in the glove compartment," Dino said. "Is there anything else in there?"

Stone removed a thick black envelope and pulled a tab that broke the seal. He shook out the contents onto the glove box door and looked at the four plastic cards that came out.

"Okay, we've got two White House passes marked 'Staff,' and two wallets with CIA ID cards." He handed one of each to Dino, who examined them.

"Looks like we clip the White House passes to our lapels. What do we do with the CIA IDs?"

"I don't know. They've never given us those before," Stone replied.

Dino clipped the White House pass to his

lapel, stuck the CIA wallet in his inside pocket, and started the car. "Oh," he said, "here's the map from the door pocket. Keep me out of trouble."

Stone opened the map and found Manassas, then found the White House. "First," he said, "drive out the gate."

Dino did so, and a minute or two later they were driving north on the interstate. "Hey," he said, "I forgot to ask where we're staying."

"At the Hay-Adams," Stone said. "Sixteenth and H Streets."

"And how do I get there?"

"It's across Lafayette Park from the White House."

"And how do I get there?"

Stone consulted the map. "Straight ahead. I'll let you know when to turn. This is your local knowledge?"

"Right. You give me directions," Dino said, "and my local knowledge will get you there."

3

They checked in, and a bellman took them to the top floor of the hotel, thence to a pair of double doors.

"We need two doors?" Dino asked.

The bellman opened the door, and they walked into a large sitting room. Stone gave the bellman a fifty. "His room is the worst one," he said, indicating Dino.

"They're both very nice," the bellman said, hesitating.

"How about the smallest bathroom?" Stone asked.

"Once again, both very nice."

"Okay," Stone said, pointing to the door on his right, "put my bags in that one."

Dino went and opened the door to his room. "Can we manage this on five hundred per diem?"

Stone shook his head. "I'm splurging. It's the first time I've spent any of Arrington's bequest. You can chip in half your per diem."

"Deal," Dino said, walking into his room. The bellman followed with his bags.

Stone went into his room, unpacked his bags, and put things in dresser drawers. He grabbed a handful of things on hangers and gave them to the bellman. "Pressed and back in an hour?"

"Better make it an hour and a half," the man said. "You've got a lot of stuff here."

Dino added some things to his burden, and the man left. Dino walked over to a set of French doors and opened them. "Wow," he said.

"Wow what?"

"Come out here and look at this."

Stone walked out and found himself on a terrace, nicely furnished. Then he looked out over Lafayette Park and saw the White House, neatly framed by trees. "Wow," he said.

"How much are you paying for this?" Dino asked.

"I don't want to know," Stone said. "I never again want to know how much anything costs."

"Let's keep this gig going as long as we can," Dino said. "How about some lunch on our terrace?"

They ordered from room service and were soon sitting on their terrace, allowing the air-conditioning to waft through the French doors to combat the August heat in Washington. They ate, and stared at the White House.

"There are people on the roof," Stone said.

"Well-armed people, no doubt," Dino replied, popping a French fry into his mouth. "And I'll bet those box things conceal ground-to-air missiles."

"Don't do anything threatening," Stone said. "They could put one right through the French doors."

"You still have no idea why we're here?" Dino asked.

"I haven't received any messages from the ether," Stone replied.

Stone was stretched out on his bed, watching MSNBC on the large flat-screen TV, when the bellman returned with his clothes and hung them in the closet.

"I hope you'll be very comfortable here," the man said, doing the bellman shuffle.

Stone gave him a twenty. "We'll struggle through," he said.

"Just let me know if you need anything at all, Mr. Barrington." The man left, taking the room service table with him.

Stone drifted off, and Holly came into his

head. He was caressing her ass when Dino rapped on the doorjamb.

"We're due over at the neighbors' house in an hour," he said. "You'd better shake your ass."

Stone reflected that that was what Holly had been doing when he had last imagined her. "Right," he said, putting his feet on the floor. "I'll grab a shower." He did so, freshened his shave, and got into clean clothes.

The valet brought the SUV under the hotel portico, and Stone walked around it once. The license plate contained only a four-digit number, 4340, and there were no manufacturer's badges on the car, just black paint. He checked out the door locks as he got into the passenger seat. "All the locks are beefy," he said as Dino got in. "And I'd be willing to bet that this is one of Mike Newman's armored vehicles. The Agency is one of his clients." Mike Newman was the CEO of Strategic Services, Stone's biggest client, on whose board he served.

"That makes me nervous," Dino said, closing his door. He looked at the key in his hand and pressed a button on it. The car started. "That makes me nervous, too. You think they think somebody's going to shoot at us or put a bomb in the car?"

"It's the CIA, Dino," Stone replied. "It's probably all they had."

They made their way to Pennsylvania Avenue. "Which gate do we use?" Dino asked.

"There," Stone said, pointing. "That's the one you see in the movies all the time."

Dino swung into the drive and stopped at the gate. Two uniformed officers wearing Secret Service badges approached, one on each side. Stone and Dino presented their White House IDs.

"Names?" an officer asked.

"Barrington and Bacchetti," Dino replied. "Sounds like a delicatessen, doesn't it?"

The officer maintained a stone face as he checked a clipboard. "Right, Mr. Barrington," he said.

"Bacchetti," Dino corrected him.

"Right. Straight ahead, under the portico. Somebody will meet you."

The gate opened and Dino drove through.

"Slowly," Stone said. "I want to take this in."

"It's not our first time here, you know." They had attended a White House dinner a couple of years before.

"I know, but I didn't take it all in that time."

Dino pulled to a stop under the portico, and a man on each side of the car opened the doors. One of them drove the car away, and the other opened the door to the building. They presented their IDs at a reception desk, and the young man who had opened the door led them down a hallway until they came to an elevator. When they got in, he pressed an unmarked button and stepped out of the car. "You'll be met," he said.

The elevator rose; Stone couldn't be sure how far. He didn't know the car had stopped until the doors opened. They stepped into a broad hallway, and a man in a dark suit with a small badge of some sort on his lapel waved them to a sofa against the wall. "Please be seated. Someone will come for you shortly."

They sat. A little way down the hall another Secret Service agent stood at a loose parade rest before a large door.

They had been on the sofa for perhaps five minutes when the elevator door opened, and the first lady of the United States stepped out, followed closely by Holly Barker. The first lady was also the director of Central Intelligence, Katharine Rule Lee, and it had taken an act of Congress to overlook the inconvenience that nepotism had been involved in her appointment.

"Mr. Barrington, Lieutenant Bacchetti," the director said, walking over and extending her hand. "It's good to see you both again."

They had already leapt to their feet to renew their acquaintance, previously made at the White House dinner.

Mrs. Lee led the way down the hall to the guarded door, which was opened for her by the Secret Service agent. "Come in," she said, sweeping into a large, handsomely furnished living room. "The president is on his way back from the West Coast and will be here in time for dinner. In the meantime, what would you like to drink?"

"Mr. Barrington will have a Knob Creek on the rocks," Holly said to a man in a white jacket, "and Lieutenant Bacchetti will have a Johnnie Walker Black the same way."

"I see you've been drinking with them," the first lady observed.

4

Stone sipped his drink slowly and had a look around. It was the living room of an upper-class American family, complete with good paintings and family photographs in silver frames on the grand piano. He wondered when somebody would get around to why he and Dino were there.

"I understand you're now a partner at Woodman and Weld," the first lady said.

"For about a year," Stone replied. "For a long time previously I was of counsel to the firm, and I worked from my home office. I still do."

"What sort of clients do you work for?" she asked.

"My largest client is Strategic Services," he said.

"I know them, of course."

"I also serve on their board."

"Mike Newman is a good man," she said. "Almost as good as his predecessor."

Stone was about to agree when the door opened, and the president of the United States breezed in, followed by a man carrying his luggage. "Good evening, all," he said.

Everyone but his wife leapt to their feet and made the appropriate greetings.

"You're early," his wife said.

"Not inconveniently so, I hope. Will you all excuse me while I get out of this suit?" Without waiting for a reply, he walked into another room and closed the door behind him.

Mrs. Lee looked at her watch. "They must have had a hell of a tailwind," she said.

"West to east will do that for you," Stone observed. "It's tougher going the other way."

"Oh, that's right, you're a pilot, and I understand you've moved up to a jet. We will want to hear about that."

"Of course," Stone replied.

"We may as well wait until he's back before I brief you."

Stone nodded. He was nursing his drink, wanting a clear head for this meeting, whatever it was about.

The president came back wearing a cardigan sweater, and the butler was waiting for him with a drink. He collapsed in a large armchair that Stone had avoided, correctly guessing it had a regular occupant.

"How was your flight down?" he asked Stone.

"Uneventful, Mr. President."

"At home, we like to be called Kate and Will," the president said. "Uneventful is the best kind. I miss flying. The Secret Service won't let me, you know. They can't get a team of a dozen agents onto my Malibu, and the required jet fighter team wouldn't be able to fly slowly enough to escort me."

"I can see the problem."

"I'm out of here in another eighteen months, though, and I've sworn to fly home to Georgia in my own airplane. Fuck the Secret Service and the Air Force."

Stone laughed. "Only you can get away with that."

"Will," his wife said, "I think I'd better get to why Mr. Barrington and Lieutenant Bacchetti are our guests this evening."

"Of course, my love, go ahead."

"Please," Stone said, "it's Stone and Dino."

She smiled, then continued. "Stone and Dino, you may recall that a year ago there was a murder on the grounds of the White House."

"I remember hearing about it on the news. The husband took his own life shortly thereafter, and was blamed for the killing."

"That is correct. Her name was Mimi Kendrick, and her husband was Brixton Kendrick. She was my social secretary, and he was, in effect, the manager of the White House, in charge of the physical plant and the office arrangements."

Stone made a note of the names.

"The problem is," the first lady said, "Will and I don't believe Brix killed his wife."

"Oh?"

She shook her head. "The investigation was, to Will's and my mind, inconclusive. Because the Kendricks were federal employees on what, in effect, is a government reservation, the D.C. police were not involved. The FBI and the Secret Service conducted the investigation. Secret Service personnel are not trained as detectives, and it's my own belief, perhaps colored by my association with the CIA, that FBI agents are not awfully good at investigating homicides, either." She looked at her nails. "It's possible that the White House staff were too willing to accept the Bureau's conclusions, given the proximity of the midterm elections. Will didn't want a stink, either, and I, in my position, was not about to publicly criticize the Bureau."

"I understand," Stone said.

Will Lee spoke up. "I'm a lame-duck

president now, and I don't really give too much of a damn about stepping on bureaucratic toes or contradicting the wise. I want to know, both for the sake of justice and for my own satisfaction, what actually occurred, and if there is a responsible person still out there, I want to see him tried and convicted."

The first lady cleared her throat. "Holly suggested that, because of your current status with the NYPD, Dino, and because you, Stone, are a retired homicide detective, and because you are both under contract to the Agency, you two might be best qualified to review the investigation quietly and draw conclusions."

"I see," Stone replied.

"We'd be glad to do that," Dino said. "Will we have access to the FBI's file on the case?"

She handed Dino a briefcase that was resting against her chair. "Everything's in here," she said. "The Secret Service file, too. Take it all with you after dinner."

"Anybody want another drink before we dine?" the president asked.

Everyone demurred.

"Good, I'm hungry."

Stone noticed that dinner had not been announced, but as soon as the president was seated, food began magically arriving. They dined on a rib roast of beef, rice, and green beans, and a bottle of good California Cabernet.

They stayed for a quick brandy after dinner, then the president rose, signaling their imminent departure. "Do you have any questions?" he asked Stone and Dino.

"Not at the moment, Mr. Pr—Will. Whom should we contact when we do?"

The first lady spoke up. "Call Holly first, and if she doesn't satisfy you, call me at my office. My secretary will know your names. If we need to meet again, we'll do it here. In the meantime, the White House staff will be apprised of your identities, and you may prowl around with an escort appointed by the chief of staff, Tim Coleman. Just call him, if you need to."

Stone and Dino said their good-byes, and Holly left with them.

When they were in the elevator, Stone asked, "Holly, what have you gotten us into?"

"After you've read the file, you can tell me," she replied. "Where did you choose to stay?"

"At the Hay-Adams."

"Nice. Are you sharing a room?"

"No, Dino has his own accommodations."

"Good, then you may invite me back for a drink," she said. "I'll drive myself and meet you there."

The elevator doors opened, and they were escorted back to the entrance, where their cars awaited.

5

Stone and Dino got out of their sinister SUV at the Hay-Adams, and Holly pulled in behind them. Stone turned to Dino. "Go to your room," he said.

"Yes, Poppa, and be sure to close your door so I can't hear your pitiful cries."

Stone opened the car door for Holly and told the valet to put it on his tab.

"Where's Dino?" Holly asked.

"He's been sent to his room."

"Oh, good."

Stone led her to the elevator and thence to the suite.

"My goodness," Holly said, "is the Agency paying for this?"

"Only to the extent of your miserable per diem," Stone replied. "Drink?"

"Oh, yes; brandy, please."

Stone poured them each one from the generous bar on the sideboard, and they sat down on the sofa, with the sight of the brightly lit White House through the French doors in the distance. Dino's door was tightly shut.

Holly set down her glass, took Stone's face in her hands, and kissed him firmly, then she picked up her glass again and took a sip. "I want to tell you some things," she said. "Personal things."

"All right," Stone said, not sure where this was leading.

"I know, perhaps better than anyone else, what you've been going through since Arrington's death."

Stone said nothing.

"You'll remember, since you were a witness to his murder during that bank robbery, that the love of my life, Jackson Oxenhandler, was taken from me in much the same way that Arrington was taken from you."

"Yes, I remember."

"I remember what I went through during the months that followed. I remember the dreams I had, the yearnings that could not be fulfilled, the pain, the constant pain. The pain, by the way, lessens after a while, then goes away."

"I'm experiencing that," Stone said, "and I feel guilty about it."

"So did I, and all I can tell you is don't

worry about it. It takes care of itself, eventually."

"I'll remember that."

"The other thing I remember vividly was how — you should excuse the expression — horny I was. I thought about sex with Jackson every time I lay down to go to sleep. After a few weeks, it surprised me that I thought about sex with you."

"That does surprise me."

"I know, we'd only just met, but some reptilian part of my brain began to distinguish between a dead lover and a potential lover who was out there, alive. So, when we finally had the opportunity, I was ready for you. And I've enjoyed every moment in bed with you since then, when we had the opportunity."

"And I with you. When you walked into Elaine's last night, I felt . . . as the song says, 'that old feeling.' "

"Good. That means you're alive and well, and you're about where I was at this stage. Do you want me now?"

Stone stroked her cheek with the back of his fingers. "Oh, yes. And I feel guilty about that, too."

"Don't," she said, taking his hand and leading him toward the open bedroom door. "Don't worry, I'll be gentle."

And she was. She undressed them both and lay in Stone's arms, caressing and kissing various parts of him. When she was ready — and when he was ready — she took him inside her, and for an hour, maybe more, they did the things they had always done with each other.

Stone was awakened by sunlight coming into his room. The curtains were open, and he could hear the shower running. He joined Holly, and they soaped and scrubbed each other, then they made love again.

Finally, they got into robes and went into the living room, where Dino was sitting in a comfortable chair, reading the *Washington Post.* "Good morning," he said. "I've ordered breakfast for us."

"How considerate of you, Dino," Holly said, kissing him on the forehead. She sat on the sofa and poured herself a glass of freshly squeezed orange juice from a pitcher already delivered by room service. "Tell me, Dino, do you have a girl these days?"

"One or two," Dino replied.

"Why don't you invite one of them down here to join you? I'm going to be taking up a lot of Stone's evenings, and I wouldn't want you to feel neglected."

Dino looked over the top of his newspaper. "That's a very good idea," he said. "Does she get per diem, too?"

"From you, not from the Agency."

"I'll make a call after breakfast."

The doorbell rang, and room service wheeled in a large cart containing bagels, smoked salmon, sour cream, and a dish of caviar. They arranged themselves about the table and pitched in.

"I'll bet you read the files last night, didn't you?" Holly said to Dino.

"I did."

"Any conclusions?"

"I found them carefully crafted to leave no alternative to Brixton Kendrick as the murderer. His suicide must have been an enormous relief to the Bureau."

"I think you could say that," Holly agreed. "I think it was an enormous relief to everybody except the people who knew them best, who believe that Brix could never have murdered his wife."

"Stone," Dino said, "I want us to go over to the White House today and walk the route from the tennis courts to the parking lot, the one that Mrs. Kendrick took. I want to see where she died."

"Good idea," Stone said. "What did the medical examiner's autopsy report say about the cause of death?"

"Oddly, the ME's report was missing from the files."

Holly stopped chewing her bagel. "Really?"

"Really."

"I'll get on that this morning," she said.

"It could be critical," Dino said. "It often is."

"I agree," Stone echoed, "and while you're scaring up that report, see if you can find out who neglected to include it. That could be very interesting to know."

"I'll do that," Holly said.

After breakfast, Holly got dressed, and Stone noted that she wore an outfit different from the one the night before. Holly had planned ahead.

He kissed her good-bye at the door. "Thank you," he said, "for last night. You were correct in all your observations."

"I'm glad you agree," she said. "Will I see you tonight?"

"Book a table at your favorite restaurant, and come here for a drink first, say, six-thirty?"

"You're on," she said, and she was gone.

6

They arrived at the White House reception desk, and Stone and Dino flashed their IDs. "We have an appointment with Tim Coleman," Stone said to the receptionist.

A call was made. "Someone will be out for you in a moment," the receptionist said.

"We know the way," Stone replied.

"Someone will be out for you in a moment."

In not much more than a moment a young male staffer materialized in the reception area and introduced himself. Everybody shook hands. "Right this way."

They were led almost to the Oval Office and then were turned into a small waiting room outside the chief of staff's office. They could see him inside, feet on his desk, talking into two telephones, a secretary waiting with a stack of papers.

Coleman hung up one of the phones and waved them into his office. "Good," he said, "you caught me on a slow day." The phone that he had hung up rang, but he ignored it and pressed the other to his chest. He pushed a button on a console. "Fair. Come in here," he said.

A moment later, a very tall woman in a short dress entered through another door. "Stone Barrington, Dino Bacchetti, this is one of my two deputies, Fair Sutherlin."

Everybody shook hands. Stone noticed a very firm grip.

"Gentlemen," Fair said, "it's a pleasure to meet you. We all appreciate your taking the time to come down here and look into this for us."

"We're glad to be here," Stone said.

"That go for you, too, Lieutenant?" she asked.

"Yep, and call me Dino. He's Stone."

"I'm yours for the morning. What do you want to see, and who do you want to talk with?"

"We'd like to walk the route that Mrs. Kendrick took from the tennis court to the place where her body was found," Stone said.

"Of course. Come with me."

Stone and Dino said good-bye to Tim Coleman, then followed Fair Sutherlin, which Stone found to be a pleasant experience. She led them past the Oval Office and down a hallway, through a couple of doors, and out onto a walkway, then stopped after a few steps.

"This is where I found Mimi Kendrick," Fair said.

"*You* found her?" Stone asked. "What were you doing out here?"

Fair looked a little embarrassed. "I had just finished a very heated phone conversation with a member of Congress, and when I hung up I was still angry. I came out here to get a little air and calm down."

"Why here?" Dino asked.

"It's the closest place to my office that's outside," she said, "unless of course I had gone through the Oval Office, and that's not something I make a habit of, unless I'm called in there."

Dino began looking at the ground around him, while Stone continued to talk with Fair. "Do you have a bad temper, Ms. Sutherlin?"

"Fair," she said. "And you might say I have a fairly bad temper, under some circumstances."

"What circumstances?"

"On that occasion, I was blatantly lied to by a congressman. I knew he was lying, and so did he, but he persisted."

"What else makes you angry?" Stone asked, but she was staring at Dino.

Stone followed her gaze. Dino was standing next to a flower bed, holding a flat piece of granite. "What have you got there, Dino?"

"The murder weapon, I think." He walked over to where Stone and Fair stood. "It's an edging rock, and it was out of line with the others. It appears to have blood and hair on it and what looks like a lipstick smudge." He pointed at a smear of something pink.

"And it was still there after a year? And with blood, hair, and lipstick on it?"

"It was stuck in the ground," Dino said, "under a bush. Evidence can sometimes last like that."

"And what does all this mean?" Fair asked.

"It means the murder was heat of the moment, not planned," Dino replied. "Mrs. Kendrick might have had an argument with someone she encountered, an argument that made the other person angry or frightened. The murderer grabbed the first weapon available and hit her on the head with it. At least, that's my guess at what a day in the FBI lab will determine."

"Very good, Dino," Stone said.

"And we're just getting started," Dino replied.

"I find this something of a stretch," Fair

Sutherlin said.

"Murder is always a stretch," Dino said, "and usually improbable. In this case, what could one woman have said to another that made her angry enough to kill?"

"I can't imagine," Fair replied.

"Perhaps Mrs. Kendrick threatened her," Stone said.

"Threatened her with what?"

"Perhaps she threatened to expose something that the other woman didn't want to become general knowledge."

"Like what?" Fair asked.

"That remains to be seen," Stone replied "Thank you for your help, Fair. We'll find our way out."

Fair left, and Stone turned to Dino. "How the hell did you come up with that?"

"I merely observed, my dear Watson," Dino said, affecting a terrible English accent. He produced a zipper bag and dropped the stone into it. "Now we'd better get this to the lab."

7

Stone navigated them along Pennsylvania Avenue toward Georgetown, and they began driving down tree-lined streets of town houses. "Two down on the left," Stone said, pointing to a house.

Dino invented a parking place and turned down his visor, which had a government business notice on it. They got out of the car and approached the front door. There was a discreet for sale sign attached to the wrought-iron fence enclosing the small front garden, bearing the name and number of a realtor. Stone pulled away a couple of inches of yellow crime-scene tape from the front door, then unlocked it and led the way in.

"Pretty nice," Dino said, looking around.

Stone walked into the living room and stopped. There seemed to be some pieces of furniture missing, and there were outlines on the walls where pictures had hung. "Burglary, you think?" Stone asked.

"Pretty picky burglars," Dino said, looking up. "There," he said, pointing at one of the beams across the room. "There's a mark where the rope was."

"That's, what, twelve feet up?" Stone asked.

"About. There must have been a ladder here. Maybe the burglars took that, too."

They walked around the house, checking the kitchen, which seemed to have been remodeled recently, and a comfortable study, where the bookcases were more than half empty and there were more missing-picture marks.

Stone opened a few drawers. "Pencils, paper clips, that sort of stuff. No paper, no files in the file drawers."

"Burglars wouldn't bother with that stuff," Dino said. "The family must have come into the house and lifted whatever they wanted."

A voice suddenly came from the doorway behind them. "Why not?" a man asked. "It was all ours."

Stone and Dino turned to find a young man of medium height and slim build, wearing surgeon's scrubs, standing behind them. "Are you FBI?" he asked.

Stone and Dino produced their White House IDs.

The young man looked closely at them.

"Anybody I can call to verify you are who these say you are?"

"Tim Coleman, chief of staff," Stone said. "Or Charleston Bostwick, his deputy."

"Yeah, I know them," he replied, handing back the IDs.

"You have us at a disadvantage," Stone said.

"Oh, sorry, I'm Tom Kendrick. They were my parents."

"We're sorry for your loss," Stone said.

"Losses," Tom replied. "The whole thing was screwy."

Stone pointed at a leather sofa. "Why don't you sit down and tell us about it?"

Tom didn't move. "What is your purpose here?"

"Some people at the White House were not satisfied with the investigation into your parents' deaths," Stone replied. "They asked us to look into it."

Tom went to the sofa and sat down, while Stone and Dino took chairs. "And what are your qualifications for that work?"

Dino spoke up. "I'm a detective lieutenant on the NYPD," he said. "Stone is a retired homicide detective."

"Then I guess you're qualified. Actually, I'm glad you, or somebody like you, is looking into the situation, because it's completely crazy."

"Tell us about it," Dino said.

"First of all, who would want to kill my mother? No sweeter human being ever existed. She had no enemies, not even in politics. And my father was just not the type to kill either my mother or himself. He's the type who would have been all over the cops until they caught the killer. He met with the FBI and Secret Service people and answered every question, broken up as he was."

"Being broken up is enough to cause some people to take their own lives," Stone pointed out. "And being a suspect in the murder of a loved one could push a lot of people over the edge."

"I guess all that is right, in theory," Tom replied. "But it doesn't jibe with who they were."

"Well," Dino said, "that's enough of a reason for us to be here. Tell me, what happened to all the things that have obviously been removed?"

"My wife and I removed them and took them to our apartment," Tom replied. "I'm a last-year resident at Washington Metro Hospital, and my wife works in a government office, so we couldn't afford to keep this house. I doubt we could pay the taxes.

We took the things we could use, or that were of sentimental value to us, and put the house on the market."

"How long ago?" Stone asked.

"Ten months," Tom replied. "The market is moribund for all the usual reasons, and it probably won't come back until the change in administrations. That always causes a huge upswing in Georgetown house sales, what with people leaving Washington and others moving in."

"May I ask what the value of the house is?" Stone asked.

"We were told it would bring four and a half, five million in better times, and maybe three and a half, four million if we can hang on until the change of administrations, which is another year and a half. Or we could take a lowball offer now. We've had a couple of those."

"What's upstairs?" Stone asked.

"Four bedrooms and baths, a smaller study for my mother, and a kitchenette."

Stone nodded. "I'm not all that familiar with the market here," Stone said, "but it sounds like you got good advice from your realtor. What was the estate worth in toto?"

"Six and a half million," Tom said. "More than half of that is this house, which they owned for more than thirty years. There was no estate tax last year, some legislative quirk."

"I'm familiar with that," Stone said. "Did you consider moving into the house until it sold? At least you wouldn't be paying rent."

"I pointed that out to Kath, but she's spooked by the fact that my father hanged himself in the living room."

Stone nodded. "By the way, how did he get a rope tied to that beam?"

"He used an eight-foot stepladder. It's in the garden shed."

Stone nodded.

Dino spoke again. "Was there anything going on in the life of either of your parents that might have been a factor in what happened?"

Tom looked puzzled. "What sort of thing are you talking about?"

"Anything unusual, out of the ordinary. Could either of them have been having an affair?"

Tom emitted a short laugh. "They had been married for nearly forty years," he said. "Since college. Doesn't seem likely at this stage of the game, does it?"

"I guess not," Dino said.

"What really gets me about this," Tom said, "is that they *both* died within a day of each other, both violently. I just can't come up with a scenario that would account for that. It will haunt me for the rest of my life." He got to his feet. "I have to go to work." He handed Dino a card. "My cell number is there," he said. "Please call me if there's anything else I can tell you, and please, *please* call me if you start to make any sense of this."

Stone and Dino shook his hand and walked him to the front door.

"Well," Dino said when he had gone, "forty years of marriage doesn't mean a lot if one partner gets the love bug up his ass, does it?"

"You're right," Stone said, "but I don't think we should explain that to Tom, unless we can prove it."

Dunn Public Library

8

Stone and Dino had a four o'clock appointment with the deputy director of the FBI, a man named Kerry Smith, who, they had been told, was the Bureau's supervising agent for the investigation into the deaths of Brixton and Mimi Kendrick. They presented themselves in his reception room on time and were kept waiting for ten minutes. As they were shown into Smith's office, Stone saw a door closing on the other side of the room.

"Good afternoon," Smith said. "I've been expecting a visit from you gentlemen." He indicated a seating area away from his desk. "Please sit down and be comfortable."

Everyone settled into chairs. "I understand that someone at the White House is not happy with the conclusions reached by our investigators."

"I think you might say that," Stone replied equably. "Why do you think that is?"

"You're asking *me?*" Smith said with a chuckle. "Why don't you ask whoever sent you to see me?"

"I just wondered if you feel that the Bureau's investigation might have left something to be desired."

"I visited the crime scene myself, less than an hour after the body was discovered, and I have seen every investigative report my agents submitted. I haven't seen any lack of enthusiasm for the investigation or any reason to question its conclusions. Now, please, tell me how I can help you."

Dino opened his briefcase and extracted a brick inside a zippered plastic bag. He set it on Smith's coffee table.

"What is that?" Smith asked.

"The murder weapon," Dino replied.

"A brick?"

"Clearly. It has blood and hair on it and who knows what else? Maybe a trace of something from the killer."

"Where did you get it?"

"It was one of many lining the flower beds adjacent to the site of the murder — the closest one to the body, as it happens. Your medical examiner's report states that the murder weapon was a blunt instrument. Your agents failed to check the nearest blunt instruments available to the killer."

Smith colored slightly. "That is embarrassing," he said.

"We'd like it run through the famous FBI crime laboratory," Dino said, "at the earliest possible moment."

Smith picked up the phone on the coffee table and pressed a button. "Shelley, will you come in for a moment, please?"

A moment later the door opened and a quite beautiful blond woman entered. "Shelley, this is Mr. Stone Barrington and Lieutenant Dino Bacchetti. Gentlemen, this is Assistant Director Shelley Bach."

Stone and Dino rose and shook her hand.

Smith picked up the plastic bag gingerly and handed it to his colleague. "Will you please hand-carry this to the lab? It may be the murder weapon in the Emily Kendrick case. Have them analyze the blood and hair on the brick for a match to Mrs. Kendrick and check the remainder of it for any possible traces of the murderer. Please impress upon the director of the lab the urgency of the situation. I'd like a report first thing tomorrow morning, even if it requires an all-nighter of the technician."

"Yessir," the woman said, and left the room.

Stone somehow knew immediately — he wasn't sure how — that Kerry Smith and

Shelley Bach were sleeping with each other, and probably had been for some time.

"That's a very valuable piece of evidence," Smith said. "I apologize for the negligence of my agents in not discovering it, and I thank you for bringing it in. What else can I do for you?"

"Mr. Smith," Stone said, "we've noticed in our reading of the Bureau's report that immediately upon the suicide of Brixton Kendrick, your agents stopped considering other possible suspects. Surely there must have been others under consideration."

"Possibly," Smith replied.

"May I ask, who were they? It might be useful for us to talk to them."

"I'm aware that no other possible suspects were mentioned in the report, and it's my assumption that the investigating agents were concerned that any such persons would almost certainly be employed in the White House, and they didn't want to call media attention to specific persons there, since that might adversely affect those persons' ability to do their jobs."

"That was very delicate of them," Stone said. "Perhaps we could speak to the agent or agents who made the decision to withhold those names from the report, and they could tell us directly, so that we might talk with the relevant people."

Smith looked at the floor. "I must tell you that such a list would have to include virtually everyone working or present near the Oval Office at the time." He cleared his throat. "Including the president of the United States."

"I think it is unlikely that the president would be a credible suspect, since it is at his behest that we are here. If he murdered Mrs. Kendrick, he would be unlikely to personally reopen the investigation a year later."

"I cannot but agree," Smith said. He picked up the phone again and pressed a button. "Shelley, when you return to your office, please consult your notes and bring me a list of all the West Wing personnel who might have had access to the crime scene around the time of the murder." He hung up. "Assistant Director Bach was the lead investigator," he said.

It seemed to Stone that Deputy Director Smith relied on Assistant Director Bach for a great many things.

"I've left a message on her voice mail," Smith said, "since she apparently has not returned from the lab as yet. Do you have any other questions?"

"I think we might have a few of Assistant

Director Bach," Stone said.

Smith looked at his watch. "Where are you staying?"

"At the Hay-Adams." Stone gave him the suite number.

"Given the hour, I think it might be best if, when she returns from the lab, I ask Assistant Director Bach to hand deliver her list to you there. Would that be satisfactory?"

"Yes," Stone replied, "it would. We'll look forward to speaking with her."

He and Dino thanked Smith for his courtesy and left.

Back at the Hay-Adams, Dino took a sip of his scotch. "You know," he said, "this investigation was played very close to the vest by the Bureau."

"Yes, it was."

"So much so that it's almost as if someone important above the agents issued them their instructions and accepted their conclusions."

"That's a very astute observation, Dino," Stone said, sipping his Knob Creek. "And it would seem that there were very few people at the White House in a position to do that, if you exclude the president and the first lady."

"And their names should be on the list that the lovely Assistant Director Bach is bringing us," he said. The phone rang, and Dino picked it up and listened. "Please send her right up," he said, then hung up.

"Well," Dino said, "I guess we'd better put on our shoes and jackets and tighten our ties."

9

Stone and Dino had made themselves presentable by the time Assistant Director Shelley Bach arrived at the door, and, as it turned out, she had made herself very presentable, too. She was wearing a black sheath under a silk coat, very high heels, diamond studs in her ears, and an expensive-looking diamond-like necklace around her throat.

"Good evening," she said, as Stone held the door for her. She shook both their hands and her hand seemed to linger in Dino's for a moment.

"Please have a seat," Stone said. "May I get you a drink?"

Bach glanced at her Cartier wristwatch. "Thank you, yes. A vodka martini on the rocks, please."

Stone turned to make the drink, and when he turned back Bach and Dino were sharing the small sofa. He delivered her drink on a small silver tray, then made Dino and himself another. Stone sat down in a chair facing the sofa and watched her take a grateful gulp of her martini.

"Long day?" he asked, by way of small talk.

"It's always a long day at the Bureau," she replied. "Especially since I was promoted."

"How long have you been an assistant director?" Stone asked.

"About three months. When Kerry was promoted from assistant to deputy director, he brought me up with him. We've worked quite closely together for a couple of years."

"What sort of cases do you work?" Dino asked.

Bach turned her body toward him as she answered. "Kerry's purview is domestic criminal investigations, so just about everything under that umbrella. I must say, though, that the Kendrick affair was the first homicide I investigated in more than four years."

"Was it?" Stone said, noncommittally.

She rolled her eyes. "I must apologize for my inattention to the bricks. That was inexcusable, and I'm very embarrassed."

"Don't worry about it," Dino said, patting her knee.

Stone observed this action with concealed

amusement. Was Dino making a move?

"You're very kind," she said. "We should have the lab report first thing in the morning, and I'll be sure to get it to you quickly." She opened the small satin clutch she had brought and extracted a folded sheet of paper, then she unfolded it and read from it: "These are the people who were in the proximity of the crime scene at the time of the murder: the president of the United States; the vice president of the United States; the secretary of state; two undersecretaries of state; the president's chief of staff, Tim Coleman; one of his two deputies, Charleston Bostwick; and two Secret Service agents."

"That's quite a list of suspects," Stone said.

"Those were the people in the Oval Office," she said, "and 'suspects' is your word, not mine. Within a short distance of the Oval Office were the president's three secretaries, the chief of staff's two secretaries, the second deputy chief of staff, Herman Wilkes, his secretary, and the secretary of Ms. Bostwick." She handed the list to Dino. "I'm sorry," she said to Stone, "I didn't bring a second copy."

"Quite all right," Stone said. Dino read the list, then handed it to Stone.

"For your information, we have, through interrogation and questioning of all these people, excluded as suspects those present in the Oval Office at the time, and all the others near the Oval Office, with the exception of Herman Wilkes, who left his office about the time of the murder to attend a meeting in the Map Room, just down the hall from the O.O. We were unable to immediately exclude him, until we had interviewed two people at the meeting who accounted for the time of his presence there."

"Did you take a look at a list of visitors to the White House at that time?" Dino asked.

"Yes, we did, and we were able to exclude all of them, since none had access to the portico."

Stone spoke up. "Were you present when Brixton Kendrick was interviewed?"

"Yes, I conducted the interview."

"What were your impressions of him at that time?"

"Very broken up, understandably. I also inferred a heavy undercurrent of guilt, and in retrospect, I think that was because he caused her death."

"When was his body discovered?" Stone asked.

"The morning after the murder," Bach replied. "His daughter-in-law stopped by the house to deliver a birthday present to him — she had a key — and she discovered the body hanging in the living room. He had kicked over the ladder he used to tie the rope to the rafter."

"Did you consider that it might not have been suicide?" Stone asked.

"We viewed his death as a homicide from the beginning of the investigation and determined it to be a suicide only after a thorough examination of the premises revealed no evidence of another person present at the time. Then there was the note, of course."

"Note?" Stone said, surprised.

"It's in the report you were given."

Stone picked up the report from the coffee table and leafed through it. "Ah, here it is. I missed it the first time."

"Read it to us," Dino said.

"It's handwritten, hurriedly, I would say: 'I take full responsibility for my wife's death and for everything that's happened. There is no life for me now, and my affairs are in order.' "

"That seemed to cover everything," Bach said. "We closed the investigation two days after his body and the note were found."

Stone read from the note again: " 'I take full responsibility for my wife's death and for everything that's happened.' He doesn't say he killed her, and what does 'everything that's happened' mean? What else happened?"

"My assumption is that he was referring to the events in his marriage that led up to the murder of his wife, and I disagree with your interpretation of 'I take full responsibility for my wife's death.' "

"I think your interpretation is a reasonable one," Dino said.

Bach nodded. "I think that, coming from as well-educated and as articulate a man as Brixton Kendrick, 'full responsibility' means 'full responsibility.' "

"I can't mount a cogent argument against your view," Stone admitted. "However, nobody we've talked to was aware of any events in the marriage that might have led to a murder/suicide. They've been pictured as the happiest and most well-adjusted of couples."

"People of their social class do not easily share the details of their marriage with others, even their peers," Bach said. "Perhaps especially not with their peers."

Stone shrugged. "If I've learned anything in my life, it's that nobody can ever understand what goes on in somebody else's marriage."

"Well said," Bach replied. She glanced at her watch. "I'm due at a cocktail party at the British Embassy," she said. "Would you gentlemen like to come along?"

"Love to," said Dino, without hesitation.

"Thanks," Stone said, "but I think I have a date with room service. You two have fun."

Dino and Bach left, and Stone thought that neither of them seemed at all broken up about his staying home.

He called Holly.

10

Stone slowly brought Holly to a climax, and continued his ministrations until she stopped twitching, then he moved up a few inches and rested his cheek on her belly.

Holly's breathing became normal. "I had forgotten how good you are at that," she said, running her fingers through his hair.

"And I had forgotten how good a pillow you are," Stone replied.

She pulled him up by his ears until his head rested between her breasts. "Have two," she said.

"Gladly."

"So what do you make of Dino's running off with Shelley Bach?" Holly asked. "The word is that she and her boss, Kerry Smith, have been an item since before the last presidential election. Do you know their story?"

"Nope," Stone sighed.

"They were assigned to find out if Martin

Stanton, whom Will Lee had picked as his vice presidential candidate, was actually born in the United States."

"I remember something about that, but I'm not sure what."

"They determined that his mother, who was Mexican, gave birth to him in an ambulance shortly after they crossed the border, on the way to a maternity hospital in San Diego."

"But he had an American father, didn't he? Would it have mattered on which side of the border he was born?"

"I have no idea," Holly said, "but you can be sure the Republican right wing would have had a field day with it."

"I suppose so."

"Where did you say Dino went with Bach?"

"To a cocktail party at the British Embassy. Why, do you miss them?"

She slapped him lightly on the cheek that was not pressed to her breast. "Don't be a smart-ass."

"Listen," Stone said.

"Listen to what?"

"I think I heard the front door open."

"And I think I heard Dino's door close," Holly said, giggling. "Who knew Dino was such a swordsman?"

"Dino does all right with the ladies," Stone said.

"Is this going to make for an embarrassing breakfast meeting?" she asked.

"It won't embarrass me."

"It might embarrass Shelley, to see me here."

"So, let's embarrass her."

"Where do you stand on your investigation?" Holly asked, changing the subject.

"Oh, you want to talk dirty now, do you?"

She slapped his cheek again. "Just give me your opinion."

"Well," Stone said, "we haven't been able to prove that Brixton Kendrick didn't murder his wife, and, I must say, it was very unhelpful of him to leave a note taking responsibility for her death. Somehow, you didn't mention that."

"It was in the report I gave you."

"Yes, I finally found it, after I had been told it was there."

"Don't blame me."

"Why not? I'm certainly not going to blame myself."

"I didn't expect you to," she laughed.

"Somehow, I don't necessarily equate his taking full responsibility with a confession of murder."

"The FBI does," Holly said.

"Shelley mentioned that," Stone said. "Of course, the FBI wants desperately for it to be true, because that way they don't have to find a murderer."

"Have you got a candidate for that title?"

"Well, I don't believe it was the president, the vice president, or the secretary of state — or either of the secretary's associates," Stone said.

"That's very patriotic of you."

"Each of them has the others for an alibi, and that's tough to shake."

"You have a point," Holly said.

Stone crawled up the bed and rested his head on the pillow next to Holly's. "Dino found the murder weapon, though." He told her about the brick. "We'll get the lab report in the morning, so I guess we can hope the murderer spat or bled or sweated on it."

"That would certainly simplify things, wouldn't it?" Holly said.

"Yes, but life is rarely that simple, and murder, even more rarely."

"Can I quote you on that? Or are you stealing from Sherlock Holmes?"

"That was entirely original," Stone said, "or at least, I can't remember anybody else ever saying that, and I haven't read Sherlock Holmes since about the eighth grade."

Holly didn't reply, and her breathing had

become slow.

Stone's breathing followed hers, and shortly, he was asleep, too.

Stone and Holly appeared for breakfast in robes and found Dino and Shelley, in robes, already attacking their meal.

"We ordered for you, too," Dino said.

"Good morning, Holly," Shelley said, without apparent embarrassment.

"Good morning, Shelley, Dino," Holly replied, shaking out her napkin and pouring herself and Stone some orange juice. "I hear your conclusions in the investigation are holding up."

Shelley nodded. "I expected them to, thank you."

"Don't thank me," Holly said. "This wasn't my idea. Actually, Stone and Dino were my idea, but only after I had my orders."

"I like your choice of investigators," Shelley said, pulling Dino's earlobe.

"So do I," Stone said, helping himself from a platter of scrambled eggs and bacon.

"Then nobody has any complaints?" Holly asked.

"I didn't say that," Stone replied. "First, I want to see the lab report on the brick."

Shelley got up and went to a telephone,

held a brief conversation, then hung up and came back to the table. "The lab report is on my desk," she said.

"And?" Dino queried.

"The blood on the brick is that of Emily Kendrick, so we have the murder weapon."

"Okay," Stone said. "What else?"

"There was no deposit of DNA by another individual," Shelley said.

"Shit!" Dino muttered.

"However," Shelley said, making sure she had everybody's undivided attention before continuing, "there was something else deposited."

Everybody stared at her in silence, waiting for the news.

"Lipstick," Shelley said. "Don't you want to know what kind of lipstick?"

"I'm just dying to know," Dino replied.

"Pagan Spring," Shelley said, "from a house brand made for a national drugstore chain."

"What's a Pagan Spring?" Dino asked.

"In this case," Shelley said, "pinkish."

"Pinkish?"

"Not exactly pink, but pinkish."

Stone interrupted. "I take it this is a cosmetic used by potentially tens of thousands of women in the D.C. area?"

"Indeed," Shelley said.
"Shit!" Dino said again.

11

Holly and Shelley had left the suite, and Stone and Dino were on their second cups of coffee. The phone rang, and Stone got it. "Yes?"

"I'm calling for Director of Central Intelligence Katharine Rule Lee," a woman's voice said. "To whom am I speaking?"

"This is Stone Barrington."

"Director Lee would be pleased if you and Lieutenant Bacchetti could join her for lunch in her dining room today at twelve-thirty."

"Please tell her we'd be pleased to join her," Stone said.

"Thank you, Mr. Barrington. There'll be visitors' passes for you at the main gate. Would you like directions?"

"Yes, please." Stone wrote everything down, thanked her, and hung up. "I hope you and Assistant Director Bach haven't planned a matinee for today," he said to Dino.

"Funny you should mention it," Dino said. "I was just thinking about that."

"Director Lee has invited us to lunch at the Agency."

"No kidding? I've never been there."

"Neither have I, but I have directions," Stone replied, waving a piece of paper.

Entry to the Central Intelligence Agency's grounds was very much like entry to the White House grounds. They gave their names at the gate, were checked off a list, then given visitors' passes and directed to a parking spot. They were met on the ground floor by a fiftyish woman who introduced herself as Director Lee's assistant and led them through the security gate and to an elevator, along the way passing a wall where nameless stars represented agents who had lost their lives in the line of duty.

The director's dining room was pleasant, paneled in a light wood, and featured a large window with a view of the woods surrounding the building. Holly was already there, sipping fizzy water.

"Why, Mr. Barrington, Lieutenant Bacchetti, what a surprise to bump into you," she said gaily.

Before they could respond, the director breezed into the room, followed by her assistant, who was jotting notes on a steno pad. "And tell them to be quick about it," Kate Lee said, then took a seat at the table, waving the others to chairs. "I'm very much afraid that this is not going to be a very good lunch," she said, "because I'm on a diet, and you have to suffer along with me."

A small salad of some sort of leaves, splashed with lemon juice, was served.

"All right," the director said, after they had begun to eat.

Stone recited what they had learned so far, which he knew would not please her, but she perked up when he came to the brick with the lipstick on it.

"Tell me," she said, "how do you think lipstick got to be on the brick? Did the murderer kiss it?"

Her question was met with silence.

"Maybe Mrs. Kendrick was wearing it," Dino said hopefully.

"No," Holly replied. "She had just come from a tennis date."

"Well," the director replied, "I have played tennis with women who were wearing lipstick, but Mimi Kendrick never wore makeup at all. She had this glowing skin that cosmetics had never touched, and she looked great."

"The lipstick does suggest that the murderer was a woman, though," Stone said.

"Or a transvestite," the director murmured.

Holly couldn't resist laughing. "At the White House? That would be something!"

"Yes," the director said, "it would be something, but you're right, Stone, it's hard to come to any other conclusion but that the murderer was a woman."

"Or," Dino said, "a man with a tube of lipstick who left some on the brick, just to drive us crazy."

"That would indicate premeditation," Stone said, "but a brick is not a weapon of premeditation, just the first thing the murderer could lay his or her hands on."

"Stone's right," Dino said. "A premeditator would bring a knife or a gun."

"Not at the White House," Holly pointed out. "He — or she — would never be able to get a weapon past security."

Everybody was quiet again.

Stone finally spoke up. "Of the people on the FBI's list of those in the area, six were women: Charleston Bostwick, one undersecretary of state, one Secret Service agent, and the president's three secretaries. And they all have unimpeachable alibis."

They waited while a waiter took away their salad plates and replaced them with dinner plates, each containing a spoonful of a green substance and a single lamb chop.

"Well, there is one helpful thing about this information," the director said, finally. "I never knew Brix Kendrick to wear lipstick."

After lunch, Holly walked Stone and Dino down to the lobby, and the three paused at the front door.

"Dinner tonight?" Stone asked Holly.

"I can't tonight," she said, "but I'm glad you two got to visit the building."

"I'm not glad," Dino replied.

"What, Dino, you didn't like being on a diet?"

"It's not that, it's the lipstick."

"What do you mean?" Stone asked.

"Before the lipstick," Dino replied, "we had an easy out. If we couldn't find a murderer, all we had to do was endorse Shelley's report, and we were out of here."

"Not anymore," Stone agreed.

"Holly," Dino said, "could you recommend a diner, or something, on the way back to the city? I'd like to stop for some lunch."

12

Dr. Josh Harmon reported to his trauma center at half past one for his two-to-twelve shift. He looked over the charts of patients seen but not admitted during the morning shift. He was pleased with the decisions made by his staff, and he posted a handwritten note on the bulletin board congratulating them on no unnecessary admissions and overall good judgment.

Josh got into clean scrubs, secured his locker, and walked into the treatment room to see a gunshot wound in a young Hispanic male. The boy was fortunate that it had passed through the upper arm muscle without striking bone, but he had lost some blood, and Josh put on a surgical mask and was gloved, while he called for the administering of one unit of whole blood.

He had just begun to work on repairing the wound when a woman in her late thirties appeared, complaining of abdominal pain. He was immediately struck by how familiar she looked, but for the life of him he could not place her. Something was different from his memory, but he couldn't put his finger on it. He looked up often as he worked, trying to jog his memory, but to no avail. The woman was diagnosed with severe constipation and was sent to a curtained booth for an enema, then he forgot about her.

Josh finished with his suturing and left an intern to dress the wound and issue a sling to the young man, before discharging him, and Josh dealt with two more patients before his break. He was sitting in the coffee room with a hot cup when it hit him: Orchid Beach. He and Holly had had dinner with the woman and a man, and he couldn't remember either of their names.

When his break was over he went back to the treatment room and found the woman's chart. Her name was Jessica Smith, with a La Jolla address, but he knew the name wasn't right. She remained on his mind for the rest of the afternoon, and it was driving him crazy. Then, during his dinner hour, he decided to put an end to it. He went to a pay phone and called Holly's direct line at the Agency.

"Holly Barker," she said.

The sound of her voice got to him; he hadn't been expecting that. "Hi, it's Josh," he said, finally.

"Well, hello there," she said. "How are things in San Diego?"

"Going better than I could have expected at this stage," he replied. "How about you?"

"Oh, you know how the work goes — win some, lose some. Lose more than I would like."

"Has Lance got the director's job yet?"

"Not yet," she said, but said no more.

"Okay, I'm sorry, I shouldn't have said that on an Agency line."

"It's okay," she said.

"Reason I called is, I saw a woman in my trauma unit today who came in complaining of abdominal pain. Turned out all she needed was an enema."

"Hey, you get all the exciting cases, don't you?"

He laughed. "She wasn't my patient, but I thought I recognized her. It drove me crazy all day, and finally I placed her."

"Josh, you didn't call to tell me about an old flame, did you?"

"No, I didn't. In fact, if anything, she's *your* old flame, in a way. You remember that couple we had dinner with at a little beach house? The guy was a great cook, and for some reason I can't even remember his face, but I remembered hers, so I checked her chart for her name, and it wasn't the right one."

"Wasn't the right one?"

"No, it wasn't her real name, but I can't remember it. Surely you remember her — the two left town suddenly."

Holly took in a sharp breath. "Lauren Cade!"

"Yes, that's it! And what was his name?"

"I don't remember," Holly said, "but it was a false name anyway."

"I don't understand."

"And I can't explain it to you, Josh, you know the drill. What name was Lauren Cade using?"

"Jessica Smith. You want her address?"

"Yes, please."

Josh dictated it to her from memory. "It's near the beach in La Jolla. I know the area."

"Thank you very much, Josh. Now, you'll have to excuse me, I'm late for a meeting."

"Nice talking with you," he said.

"Same here."

Josh hung up and went back to work, relieved of the necessity of remembering the woman's name, but now he had Holly's voice in his head.

■ ■ ■ ■

Holly looked in her computer for Todd Bacon's satphone number and rang it. The ringing was interrupted by a loud beep.

"It's the office," Holly said. "Stand by to write. We have a Lauren Cade sighting in San Diego. Here's an address in La Jolla." She recited what Josh had given her, then hung up.

Ten minutes later her phone rang. "Holly Barker."

"It's Bacon. How recent is this information?"

"Early this afternoon, local time. She turned up at a trauma center complaining of abdominal pain and was given an enema and discharged."

"Thanks for that image," Todd said.

"You're welcome."

"You have no way of knowing if the address is good?" he asked.

"That's why you're out there, bub," she said. "Get back to me when you know the answer to that question, and when you do, have a plan." She hung up.

13

Teddy Fay woke suddenly. Something — a noise, maybe — had startled him. He tried replaying whatever he had been dreaming and realized it was a gunshot that had wakened him, one that he had fired at some shadowy figure in his dream.

Teddy lay back in bed and slowed his breathing. Something was still wrong. His girlfriend, Lauren Cade, stirred beside him. "You awake?"

"Yes," he said, "something woke me."

"What — noise? Doorbell?"

"Something else. It's happened before. I've learned not to ignore it." Teddy had been a fugitive for years now, and he had remained free because he listened to this sixth sense. It was as if someone had unexpectedly tapped him on the shoulder and said clearly, "It's time to go."

Teddy got out of bed, took the Colt Government .380, which was a miniature of the .45 Model 1911, and slowly began to walk the perimeter of the little beach house in La Jolla, a San Diego suburb. He and Lauren had left Santa Fe after a CIA officer had tracked them down there. They had been safe and happy in La Jolla for more than a year, but they had to run.

He went, barefoot and silent, from room to room without turning on any lights. There was half a moon that night, and as he looked out every window in its turn, he could spot no one. He went back to the bedroom, where Lauren was sitting up in bed. "It's time to go," he said.

"Teddy, are you sure? Do you know something I don't?"

"No, I'm not sure. The only way to be sure is if someone sticks a pistol in my ear and cuffs me. And I don't know anything you don't, except that I do. I just do."

"All right," she said.

"Are you with me, sweetie?" he asked. "You can always bail out, if you're tired of this."

"I'm with you," she said. "I'm not tired of *you.*"

"All right," Teddy said, looking at the luminous hands on his watch. "We have to be out of here in one hour — say, three o'clock. That's an hour and five minutes.

Start with what you absolutely cannot bear to leave behind, then widen your circle to include the less essential but important. We're not going to turn on any lights. We're going to load the car with the garage door closed and head out."

Lauren started dressing.

Teddy started with his computer equipment — a MacBook Air — and his printer, and two magic boxes he had built himself and was thinking about marketing. He could forge any document, break into any database, with those. He always kept the original packaging for important things, and he located the boxes and manuals in the dark. Next came his tool kits and weapons — a silenced sniper rifle in a briefcase that he had designed and made for the CIA during the twenty-odd years he had served in the Agency's Technical Services department. They didn't know that he had made a duplicate rifle for himself.

He went to the sixty-inch safe, opened it, and took out the handguns and the cash. He already had cases ready for everything. He loaded all these things and put them into the SUV, then he climbed on top of the vehicle and unscrewed the bulb that normally came on when the garage door opened.

He went back to the bedroom and began throwing clothes into a suitcase. "How are you coming?" he asked.

"Pretty well," she replied, packing a bag. "I'll be ready by three."

"Sooner, if you can," he said, handing her a pair of latex gloves and pulling some on himself. "I'm going to start wiping down the house."

He started with the bedroom, then went to the bath and kitchen, then to the rest of the house, spraying things with alcohol-and-water window cleaner and wiping with a clean dishcloth. When he finished, Lauren's things were in the SUV, and she was ready. They got into the car.

"Ready?" he asked, handing her a SIG Sauer P239. "There's one in the chamber."

"Ready," she said.

He switched off the auto-on interior lights. He touched the remote control, and the garage door rose silently. He had aligned and greased it carefully for such a moment. "Let's give it a push," he said.

They both opened their doors and got the vehicle rolling, then got back in. As the car rolled down the driveway, he touched the remote again to close the garage door. He had chosen the house, in part, because of the hill, and now the car rolled noiselessly down the street. He was two blocks away before he started the engine, then he used as little power as possible for another three blocks, checking the mirrors constantly for another moving vehicle. Nothing. He finally switched on the headlights.

They drove out to Montgomery Field, eight miles north of San Diego, to a never-used back gate that Teddy had cut the lock and chain off and substituted his own combination padlock. Lauren unlocked the gate and opened it, then closed and re-locked it when Teddy had driven through.

The field was dark, except for the runway and taxiway lighting. Teddy drove to their hangar, parked, and unlocked the hangar and opened the door. The two of them pushed the Cessna 182 RG out onto the ramp and quickly loaded their things into it, then Teddy put the car into the hangar, wiped it down, and closed and locked the door. Nobody would bother to look in it for at least another month, when the rent hadn't been paid. If he had had more time he could have sold it, but what the hell? He could eat the loss.

Teddy had a good look around the field and saw nothing moving. The tower was closed, as takeoffs were discouraged between eleven-thirty P.M. and six A.M. He ran through the checklist quickly, then started the engine, waiting only a moment before moving to be sure it was running smoothly. He taxied across the ramp and straight onto the short runway, 28 Left, at a point that left him 2,000 of its 3,400 feet, more than the airplane needed to get off the ground. Leaving the airplane's lights and transponder off, he pushed the throttle to the firewall, waited for seventy knots, then rotated. He leveled off at 200 feet, then turned inland.

He had recently installed a Garmin flat screen that was capable of Synthetic Vision, a GPS-generated map of the world that displayed high terrain and obstacles. When he was well inland, he began to climb, so as to clear the Santa Monica Mountains east of Los Angeles. When they had crossed the peaks, he turned north over the desert, avoiding the restricted area surrounding Edwards Air Force Base, on a dry lake bed.

Teddy finally spoke for the first time. "How does San Francisco sound?" he asked.

"Sounds good," Lauren said. "Do you think you were right about your feeling?"

"I think so," Teddy said. He altered course, but something still nagged at him. "No," he said, "not San Francisco. They'll work their way up the coast, checking every general aviation airport, and they'll find the airplane."

"But it has a new paint job and a new legal registration number."

"They'll be looking for a new paint job," Teddy replied.

"Then where will we go?"

"East," Teddy said, looking at his planning chart. "We'll overnight somewhere in the Midwest, then tomorrow, into the belly of the beast."

"Washington, D.C.?" she asked, incredulous.

"Near enough," he said. "Clinton, Maryland, Washington Executive Airport. As close to D.C. as we can get. They'll never think of that."

14

The team of six men let their vehicles roll silently down the hill, nearly to the house, then they got out and trotted the last thirty yards. Todd Bacon gave them the hand signal that told them to take the positions worked out during their planning session at the motel, none of them on Teddy's property, which Todd knew would have motion sensors.

When enough time had passed, Todd walked up the front walk at a normal pace, crouched before the front door, and used a professional lockpick to open it, then he unslung his light machine gun and spoke one word into his handheld radio: "GO!"

They came into the house from all sides, kicking doors open. One minute later, Todd spoke again on the radio. "They're gone," he said. He was disappointed but not terribly surprised.

"All right," he said into the radio, "let's

take this place apart. Bag anything that might be remotely of use."

The team went to work. Two hours later, they had three garbage bags full of what Todd knew was nearly all garbage. Still, there might be that one thing.

"All right," he said. "I want you to pull out all stops, yank in as many bodies and phones as you can get your hands on. I want a survey of every general aviation airport — nothing is too small — that has had land today a stranger in a Cessna 182 RG with a fresh paint job, and do callbacks from a month ago to now." Todd clapped his hands together. "Let's get to work, people." He got into his vehicle and drove back to the very nice motel that had been home for the past twelve days.

Todd dumped his bag in his suite, dug out his satphone, and walked out to the pool. It was too early for swimmers, but he'd have a clear view of the satellite. He punched in the number, and it rang.

"This is Holly Barker," she said.

"It's Todd Bacon."

"How did it go in San Diego?" she asked.

"It went extremely well," he replied.

"Does that mean you actually bagged Teddy?"

"No, that would have been super well. We missed him by, well, maybe as little as thirty minutes — four hours, max."

"Poor timing, then."

"We've been working flat-out. We couldn't take him yesterday afternoon, when you got the call from the doc in San Diego. It would have caused an uproar in the neighborhood, would have been all over drive-time news. We do *not* want to be the talk of the town on this job."

"Certainly not," Holly replied. "You were right to wait until the middle of the night. You must have spooked him somehow."

"Impossible," Todd said. "He had no idea."

"So he's in his airplane now, free as a bird."

"I'm afraid so."

"Listen, next time concentrate on finding the airplane first, then stake it out so if he runs, you'll get him at the airport."

"That's a very sensible suggestion," Todd said.

"It's not a suggestion," Holly said emphatically. "You should have thought of it earlier, instead of waiting for me to tell you."

"All right, all right. I have a good team, though, and we *are* going to get Teddy. We've already started a survey of every GA airfield on the West Coast, all the way to the Canadian border."

"Why the West Coast? I mean, apart from why not?"

"His choices were south to Mexico, north up the West Coast, or east to God-knows-where. I think he likes the West Coast, it's a very appealing place. I can't see Teddy disappearing into Kansas, you know? He has certain needs of a hometown — some arts, good restaurants, shopping. We mustn't forget that he has the girl. She's not going to rely on Walmart for her shopping."

"I know her," Holly said, "and your assumption is correct. She needs opportunities for style around her."

"Well, that sounds like San Francisco or Seattle to me — how about you?"

"Either would fit the bill, or any suburb of the two places."

"The airport is the key," Todd said. "He has to have that to make his escape when we rumble him, and we *will* rumble him. How much time have I got?"

"I want a definitive, provable, but very quiet end to this well before our man's term is up."

"That's eighteen months. Have we got that long?"

"Make it a year."

"I can do it in that time," Todd said.

"I think you can, too," she replied, "and if you can't, there's always that big pot of oil we keep on simmer down in the basement, waiting for your tender carcass." She hung up.

Todd hung up, too, and then he gulped. It wouldn't be boiling oil, he knew; it would probably be something worse.

15

Stone and Dino were having breakfast when the phone rang, and Stone picked it up.

"Mr. Barrington?"

"Yes."

"This is Fair Sutherlin."

"Good morning. You're up early."

"It's eight o'clock. I've been in my office for an hour. Oh, that's right, I forgot: you're on vacation."

Stone ignored the dig. "I'm an attorney. I keep banker's hours."

She laughed. "I'm sorry, I can't resist getting at real people, who have a business life and a private life. When you work at the White House, you have only one life, and it's here."

"You make it sound like drudgery," Stone said.

"Oh, no, it's too exciting for drudgery. It's more like combat."

"I see."

"I'm breaking out and giving a small dinner party on Saturday night," she said. "Could you both come? I'll get Mr. Bacchetti a dinner partner, if he needs one."

"Hang on," Stone said, and turned to Dino. "Fair Sutherlin wants us for dinner Saturday night. Do you want her to get you a date?"

"I already have a date," Dino said. "I'll bring her."

Stone went back to the phone. "Is a female FBI agent okay?"

"Oh, that's perfect," Fair said. "Nobody there will ever have met a female FBI agent."

"Where and what time?"

"Seven-thirty for eight." She gave him the address. "Of course, everything will be off if the country suddenly goes to hell, as it so often does. You'll be called, in that case."

"I understand," Stone said. "The country comes first."

"But not necessarily in my heart," she said. "See you then." She hung up.

"That's a surprise," Stone said.

"You're too easily surprised," Dino said. "You always were. If I'd put my mind to it, I could have predicted the invitation. She was looking at you a little hungrily back when she was a murder suspect."

"Good thing we cleared her," Stone said. "It probably would have been unethical to go out with a suspect."

"When did that ever stop you?"

"Is this the guy talking who was fucking a desk sergeant not so long ago?"

"Yeah, but she was a hot desk sergeant."

"I can't deny that. I always admired your guts, Dino. If that had come to light, you'd be walking a beat now, instead of moonlighting for the president."

"Nah," Dino said, "the commissioner and I are like that." He held up crossed fingers. "The chief of detectives wouldn't dare mess with me — at least not while he's fucking a lieutenant in the Public Affairs office."

"God, the department is a hotbed of illicit liaisons these days, isn't it?"

"So what else is new?"

"It's considerate of the chief to give you a get-out-of-jail-free card."

"Yes, it is, isn't it?"

"You'd better watch your ass if his lieutenant dumps him."

"Don't worry, I know her, she's not stupid. She knows which side of her badge gets polished."

"I'm going to try and make sense of that metaphor while I do the crossword," Stone said, picking up the *Times.*

"Good luck."
"With the metaphor or the crossword?"
"Both."
Stone folded the paper back and looked at one-across. Almost immediately, the phone rang. "Hello?"
"It's Holly."
"Hey, there."
"Did I wake you?"
"Wake me? I'm already on the crossword."
"You want to take me to a fancy restaurant on Saturday night?"
"I'd love to, but I've accepted an invitation to a dinner party at Fair Sutherlin's house."
"I'm jealous already."
"Oh, come on."
"The woman's a shark, you know."
"And she seems so nice."
"That's because she knows you're in with the president and the first lady."
"You mean she's not this nice to everybody?"
"Everybody thinks so, until they suddenly feel blood running down their necks from an open artery."
"Oh, come on."
"Are you forgetting what city you're in?"
"Is it really all that different from New York?"

"In New York, everybody thinks only of business. Here, they think about politics, and believe me, that's a whole different ball game. Every person you meet is not just out for himself, he's out for the guy he works for and the guy *he* works for. That means everybody has at least three main causes to screw other people for, and that's before you take into account the effect of partisan politics on relationships."

"So you're worried about me?"

"Listen, a simple, barefoot New York lawyer like yourself wouldn't last a week in this town. Where Washington is concerned, you're a rube, and a disposable one at that."

"Suddenly I feel naked and alone," Stone replied.

"That's rather a nice thought," she said.

"I hope to God we're not on an Agency line."

She laughed. "Give me credit for knowing when I can get away with talking dirty."

"Listen, what if I take you to a fancy restaurant tonight instead of Saturday, and we can continue this conversation over a bird and a bottle."

"Done," she said.

"You pick the restaurant and book the table. The headwaiters here don't know who I am."

"If I'm doing my job properly, they don't know who I am, either, but leave it to me."

"You going to do something sneaky to get a good table?"

"I'm sneaky for a living," she said.

"And good at it."

"You said it, pal."

"A drink here at, say, six-thirty?"

"I'm going to feel like martinis tonight," she said.

"Then I will aid and abet."

16

Teddy Fay turned the Cessna toward Clinton Field, in the southeast quadrant of greater Washington, D.C., put in a notch of flaps, and dropped the landing gear. It was sunset on their second day of flying since leaving San Diego. He reduced speed and put in full flaps. The airplane touched down lightly and taxied past the FBO (Fixed Base Operator) toward an area of hangars.

"Tell me again why we're landing at D.C.," Lauren Cade said.

"Because it's the last place Mr. Todd Bacon would think of looking for me. You can bet your sweet ass that right now he's got a team canvassing every general aviation airport on the West Coast all the way to Canada."

"I get that part," Lauren said, "but there have to be, at the very least, dozens of people in D.C. that you used to work with at the Agency who would recognize you on sight."

Teddy shook his head. "First of all, most of a generation of people I worked with have retired, and they don't have the money to move into D.C. Those who are still active live out near McLean, as close to work as they can."

"I guess that makes sense, but being here still makes me nervous."

"Why? Nobody here knows you, do they? And remember, I wear disguises," he said, pointing at the toupee that covered his pate.

"It's true," Lauren said, "that you do disguises better than anybody I ever saw. Sometimes even *I* find you unrecognizable."

"That's because I have a pretty much featureless face. A nose here, a mustache there, and I'm somebody else. So relax, baby, we're going to be just fine."

"Okay," she said.

"Besides," Teddy said, "I have a little hideaway at this airport that I kept for years as a backup to Manassas. I have a hangar here that you'll like."

"A hangar? What's to like?"

"O ye of little faith," Teddy said, stopping before a hangar. He shut down the engine, walked to the small door set into the hangar door, worked a combination lock, and stepped inside. A moment later the hangar door opened squeakily. He walked back to the Cessna, got out the tow bar, and backed the airplane into the hangar.

"We have a car," he said, pointing to an oldish Toyota parked in a corner. He closed the hangar door and switched on a light. "Grab a couple of bags," he said, "and follow me."

He grabbed some bags himself and led her up a flight of stairs, where he tapped a code into a keypad, opened a door, and switched on some lights.

Lauren looked inside. "It's a living room," she said.

"It's an apartment," he corrected. "There's a bedroom, a kitchen, and an office, too." He fiddled with the thermostat, and cool air began to flow. "We need to dust and vacuum and lay in some groceries," he said, "but that can wait until tomorrow. Let's shower and change, and I'll buy you dinner."

Stone answered the bell and let Holly into the suite, then gave her a kiss. "You look smashing," he said, admiring the tight yellow dress. "I thought CIA people were purposely drab and were trained to fade into the background."

"Once in a while I fox everybody by being noticeable," she said.

"And noticeable you certainly are." He went to the bar, opened the freezer, and removed a pitcher of martinis that he had premixed. He filled a martini glass, dropped in three olives on a spear, and handed her the glass, then poured himself a Knob Creek on the rocks. "Here's to knockout dresses on beautiful women," he said, raising his glass.

Holly took a tentative sip, then a bigger one. "Wow," she said.

"It's colder than ice."

"I noticed that." She sucked an olive off the toothpick and chewed thoughtfully. "Wow again! What's in these olives?"

"Anchovies," Stone said. "I didn't want to tell you before you tasted one. Lots of people blanch at the thought of anchovies."

"A perfect combination," she said. "It's fairly cool tonight, let's sit on your terrace."

Stone opened the door and followed her outside. She leaned against the railing and looked toward the White House. "Much of what happens in the world starts there," she said. "It never ceases to amaze me how well our government works."

"Sometimes," Stone said.

"A lot of the time, because the government is full of people like me who love the country and want it to do well."

"Does the Agency work well?"

"Again, a lot of the time. We probably make more mistakes than a lot of government agencies, but then we're working in a world that's full of surprises."

"Isn't it the Agency's job to figure out what the surprises are before they happen?"

"Then they wouldn't be surprises," she said. "Lance and I do the presidential intelligence briefings when Kate is away, and we're always able to warn him about two or three things that are about to happen."

"And then," Stone pointed out, "the Soviet Union collapses and Egypt erupts, and the Agency didn't predict those."

"The big ones are harder to predict than you'd think. We get more than our fair share right."

"I won't argue the point," Stone said.

"You'd better not, if you want hot sex tonight."

"This is my mouth closing," Stone said, making a zipping motion.

Holly tossed off her martini and popped the last olive into her mouth. "I'm hungry," she said, "and you have to feed me more than olives."

"Where are we dining?" Stone asked.

"At an old D.C. favorite," she replied. "Maison Blanche, next door to the White House, where the old guard goes, and some of the new guard, too. You'll see movers and shakers."

Stone drained his glass. "One more of these and I'll be unable to either move or shake. I hope you're driving."

"We're being driven," she said, "courtesy of the Agency. There's a little flap on, and we're battening a few hatches, just in case, and mine is one of the hatches."

"I place myself entirely in your hands," Stone said, "except that I'm still buying dinner."

"You talked me into it," she said, heading for the door.

They took the elevator to the lobby and walked out to the portico, where the usual black SUV awaited.

"I'm going to have to give you a leg up," Stone said, "what with the tight dress."

"I'll manage," she said, "and remember, don't talk shop in front of the driver — not your shop or mine."

"Didn't I already shut up?" Stone asked, opening the door for her.

17

The restaurant was not small, but intimate nonetheless. They were seated at a banquette, back-to-back with another. "I'm surprised that the place is so full at this early hour," Stone said.

"Washington, like L.A., is an early town, because everybody goes to work at the break of dawn," Holly said.

Stone ordered a second drink for them, and they relaxed. He was vaguely aware of some people being seated behind them, but his attention was on Holly. "I like you with your hair up," he said. "You have a lovely neck." He leaned over and kissed it.

"Careful," she said, "you'll attract attention."

"I'm sorry, I forgot we were being discreet. I guess that rules out what I was going to do with my hand."

"Do it later," she said. "Look across the room: see the man squeezed into the booth with that distinguished-looking couple? His name is Lyle 'Scooter' Hardin. He's a social columnist, has a blog. He'll work the room, then move on to Georgetown, and everyone will see their name online tomorrow morning."

As Stone watched, the man left the booth and crossed the room, headed directly for them.

"Watch yourself," Holly said, smiling at Stone.

Then the man was hovering over their table. "Good evening, folks," he said.

"Good evenin'," Holly replied, affecting an accent slightly more southern than her own.

"You're at the Agency, aren't you?" he asked Holly.

She looked blankly at him. "Which agency is that? There's lots of them, aren't there."

"Oh, come on, ma'am," he said. "I've seen you around."

"Have you spent much time in Atlanta lately?" Stone asked. "That's where we're from."

"Yeah, sure," Hardin said. "May I have your names for my column?"

"Column?" Stone asked. "You're with the newspapers?"

"The newspapers are dead media," Hardin replied. "The Internet is where everything's at."

"You shouldn't end a sentence with *at,*" Holly said sternly.

"Huh?"

"We don't want our names in the paper," Stone said.

"Or on the Internet," Holly chipped in.

"We don't do facetube, and we don't twit," Stone said.

Scooter smirked at him. "Sir, I don't think you're the rube you're pretending to be."

"Who are you callin' a rube?" Stone asked. "Good God, I hope everybody in Washington isn't as rude as you are."

"Please let me buy you a drink," Hardin said, swiping a chair from a nearby table and pulling it up to theirs.

"We already have a drink," Stone said, "and tonight, one's our limit."

"Now, really," Hardin said, "that gorgeous dress didn't come from Atlanta."

"*We* have a Saks Fifth Avenue," Holly said, indignantly. "At Phipps Plaza."

Scooter pointed at Stone. "That suit didn't come from off the rack at Saks," he said.

"I've got a tailor in London," Stone replied. "I'm there a lot on business."

"And what business would that be?" Hardin asked.

"None of yours," Stone said.

"Well," Hardin said, "I know the lady's at the Agency, and you're, let's see, at State?"

"Sir," Stone said, "I'm a Republican, and I find your suggestion insultin'. The lady's a Republican, too, and she has a very nice little art gallery at home."

Holly put her hand on Stone's arm. "Don't tell him any more, sugar, we don't need his kind of publicity."

Stone took a deep breath and let it out, as if he were trying to control himself. "Sir," he said to Hardin, "if you want to go on with this, you and I are goin' to have to do it outside, if you get my meanin'."

The maître d' materialized at their table. "Excuse me, sir," he said to Stone, "is this gentleman annoying you?"

"I guess you could say that," Stone replied. "Except the 'gentleman' part."

"Mr. Hardin," the man said, "I've spoken with you about this before."

Hardin threw up his hands. "All right, all right, I surrender." He beat a rapid retreat.

"I want to apologize to you both," the maître d' said.

"I'd be grateful if he didn't get my name from the reservations list," Stone said, slipping the man a fifty.

The maître d' declined the money. "Don't worry, Mr. Barrington, we will see that your privacy is respected." He bowed and left.

They ordered dinner and another drink, and suddenly, Stone picked up the words "two cops from New York" from the banquette at his back. Holly heard it, too. They stopped talking and listened to the woman's voice.

"I think this proves that Will Lee is trying to pin that murder on somebody," she said. "He's got these out-of-towners in to write a report that he's going to leak to the media, saying Brix Kendrick didn't kill his wife. And after he's already confessed!"

"It is odd," her companion replied.

"What none of the investigations has turned up is Brix's affairs," she said.

"Brix was having affairs?" her companion asked. "I don't believe it."

"Well, one of his lovers is a friend of mine, and she lives in terror that she's going to get pulled into the investigation and get her name in the paper and her husband will divorce her."

Then another couple joined the two, and the subject of their conversation changed.

Holly kept her voice low. "I don't know which is more interesting: that she knows you're in town, or that Kendrick was having affairs."

"Neither do I," Stone said. "I thought our investigation was a closely held secret."

"Well," Holly said, "it may be a secret, but it's apparently not closely held."

"Apparently not."

"You remember in the movie when somebody says to Jack Nicholson, 'Forget it, Jake. It's Chinatown'?"

"Yes."

"Well: Stone, it's Washington."

"I learn a little more about it every day," Stone said.

"Oh, by the way, don't make any plans for lunch tomorrow."

"Why not?"

"Because you're going to be invited to have it with the president."

"How do you know *that?*" Stone asked.

"Stone, it's Washington."

18

Stone and Dino were kept waiting at the White House for more than half an hour before being ushered into the Oval Office, where a waiter was setting up a table.

The president greeted them with handshakes, then they sat down. "You're having lobster salad," Will Lee said, "because I've heard you like it."

"That's entirely true," Stone said, while Dino nodded.

"I'm having something unspeakable," Lee said. "Kate has me on a diet. I mean, I exercise five days a week, I don't know why I have to be skinny, too."

"You look just fine to me, Mr. President," Dino said.

"You know, I think so, too," Lee said. "I'd order the lobster salad, but it would get back to Kate in a heartbeat."

The waiter returned with a cart and served lobster salad to Stone and Dino, then put something before the president, who grimaced. "I've learned not to ask what it is," he said.

"If it's any consolation, Mr. President," Stone said, "when we had lunch with Mrs. Lee, she had something fairly awful-looking."

"That's comforting," Lee said wryly.

"But she made us eat it, too," Dino said. "Or tried to. We had lunch at a diner later."

The president laughed heartily. "Serves her right," he said, "but don't ever let her know. You'll never hear the end of it. Wine, anyone?"

"We wouldn't dare," Stone said.

"All right," the president said, swallowing without chewing, "tell me what you've got."

"Gossip," Stone said.

"We have gossip?" Dino asked, looking confused.

"I'm sorry, Dino," Stone said, "I didn't have a chance to tell you. Mr. President, Holly Barker and I had dinner last night at Maison Blanche, and —"

"I heard she was wearing a smashing yellow dress," Lee said.

Stone's jaw dropped.

"It's Washington," the president said.

"Yes, sir," Stone said. "Well, anyway, we were sitting at a banquette, and there was another one back-to-back with us, and we overheard a conversation between a couple that was an eye-opener."

"I can't wait to hear this," Dino said.

"Dino, I said I was sorry. Anyway, Mr. President, the woman at the table said that Brixton Kendrick had had a number of affairs."

"Brix?" Lee asked, looking astonished.

"Yes, sir."

"So we're reduced to restaurant gossip?" Dino asked.

"It's the best lead we've had so far," Stone said.

"What about the lipstick?" Lee asked.

"I'm afraid that's gone nowhere, sir," Stone replied. "But it was the rest of the conversation that was interesting."

"I can't wait," Dino said.

Stone shot him a dirty look. "The woman said that a friend of hers had been having an affair with Kendrick, and that she was terrified that she would be questioned by us, and her husband would divorce her."

"By you?" the president asked. "She knew about you?"

"Mr. President, it's Washington."

Lee nodded. "So she said she actually knew someone who was having an affair with Brix?"

Stone nodded. "I thought that gave the conversation more weight than mere gossip."

"Who was this woman at the restaurant?" Lee asked.

Stone produced his notebook. "I got that from the maître d' before we left: the couple were Mr. and Mrs. Biddle Trask."

"Biddle Trask? He's the secretary of commerce. I appointed him."

"I don't know his wife's name," Stone said.

"Elizabeth — Betty. I think you'd better have a word with her, and you tell her I sent you — *personally.*"

"Yes, sir."

"My secretary will give you her address."

"Thank you, sir."

The president looked thoughtful. "That puts a whole new complexion on this affair, doesn't it?"

"Well, it's something we didn't know," Stone said.

"Or just found out," Dino said.

"I handled a few murder cases when I was a young lawyer," Lee said. "Well, one murder case. Anyway, if this information is true, then it might make Brix's suicide more understandable. He could have feared his past coming out."

"I'm afraid this information, if it's true, might go against your contention that Kendrick didn't kill his wife," Stone said.

The president nodded. "I must admit, it took the wind out of my sails. I hope I haven't gotten you two down here for nothing."

Stone didn't know what to say to that.

"Well, since the word is out that you are in town, we're going to have to be very careful here," Lee said.

"We haven't been paid anything," Stone said, "and it's not necessary that we are paid. I think it might be better if we can honestly say that we aren't on the government payroll."

The president sighed. "Dick Nixon would have had a pile of cash in somebody's safe to handle a situation like this."

"Mr. President, I think we would prefer not to be paid."

"Then I will respect your wishes in that regard," Lee said.

"There's something else to consider here," Stone said.

"What's that?"

"So far, everyone we've interviewed has been a White House staffer," Stone said. "But if we interview Elizabeth Trask, then we lend credence to her gossip."

"I take your point, Stone," Lee said, "but if you've interviewed *anybody,* then it's out there. I don't think talking to Betty will make things worse. Oh, you might tell her that I said to shut up or I'll tell her husband she's spreading this stuff."

"Mr. President, it was her husband to whom she was telling it."

"Oh, yes," Lee said. "I forgot about that. Well, Biddle Trask is not the kind to spread gossip, though I'm sure he was very interested in hearing it."

"Mr. President, as long as we're talking about Brixton Kendrick's sex life, was there anyone here in the White House that he seemed to have an unusual interest in? Any woman, I mean."

"Well, Brix wasn't gay," Lee said, "I'd bet on that. Of course, I would have bet he never had an affair with anybody."

"That's what everyone we've talked to has told us," Dino said.

"Brix ran the White House, in the nonpolitical sense," the president said. "He would have had both reason and opportunity to talk to anyone on the premises, but I can't think of anybody he seemed attracted to. Brix was a very charming guy, with both men and women."

"I understand, Mr. President," Stone said,

putting down his fork and placing his napkin on the table. "I think it's time to let you get back to running the country."

They all stood and shook hands. Stone stopped at the president's secretary's desk and got the Trasks' address, then he and Dino left.

Dino waited until they were in the car. "I can't *believe* you didn't tell me about this conversation at the restaurant," he said.

Stone sighed and fastened his seat belt. "It's a Georgetown address," he said.

19

The house was bigger than what Stone had come to expect in Georgetown. It was surrounded by lawn and gardens, and set back from the street, with a circular driveway.

"Maybe we should have called first," Dino said.

"I'd rather surprise her," Stone replied.

Dino pulled into the driveway, and they got out of the SUV and rang the bell. A uniformed maid answered the door.

"May I help you?" she asked, regarding them as if they were Bible salesmen.

"Mr. Barrington and Lieutenant Bacchetti to see Mrs. Trask, at the request of the president of the United States."

The woman blinked. "Please come in. I'll see if Mrs. Trask is at home." She showed them to chairs in a round foyer and disappeared through a door.

"At home?" Dino asked. "Doesn't she know if her boss is at home?"

" 'At home' means receiving visitors who don't have an appointment."

"Thank you for translating," Dino replied. "I think I'm going to let you handle this one. She's not used to people like me."

"Cops?"

"Italians."

The maid reappeared. "Mrs. Trask will see you. This way, please." She led them into a large room full of chintz-covered furniture and Audubon prints of birds. A handsome woman in her fifties sat alone on a sofa, looking nervous.

"Good afternoon, Mrs. Trask," Stone said. "I am Stone Barrington, and this is Lieutenant Dino Bacchetti. The president asked us to visit with you."

"Please sit down," she replied, waving a hand vaguely.

Stone and Dino chose chairs.

"Mrs. Trask," Stone said, "I know that you've heard of our presence in town and why we're here."

"How would you know that?" she asked.

"It's Washington," Stone said.

"Well, yes."

"I'm aware of your conversation with your husband at Maison Blanche last evening."

"Good God! Is the place bugged?"

"I was sitting at the banquette immedi-

ately behind yours, about two feet away."
"You were eavesdropping?"
"I was having dinner. It was impossible not to hear what you were saying."
"A gentleman would not have heard it," she said, drawing herself up to her full height.
"Be that as it may," Stone said, "I am aware that a friend of yours was having an affair with Brixton Kendrick." He took his notebook from an inside pocket and got out his pen. "The president would like you to give us her name and address."
"Good God, you can't go bursting into Muffy Brandon's house and demanding to know about her secret life!"
Stone wrote down the name. "Mrs. Trask, we are not the SWAT team. We are investigating a murder and a suicide at the request of the president of the United States, and we will exercise the utmost discretion. What is Mrs. Brandon's address?"
"How did you know her name?"
"You just told it to me," Stone said, as patiently as he could.
"Oh, my God! You see what you've made me do?"
"Please, Mrs. Trask: Mrs. Brandon's address."
The woman sighed. "She lives two houses

that way," she said, pointing. "It's the green house with the window boxes."

"Thank you. Now, last evening you said that Mr. Kendrick had had numerous affairs. With whom?"

"Well, I don't know if they were numerous," she said. "I know of only one other."

"And who would that be?" Stone asked, pen poised.

"I've heard that Milly Hart and Brix were surreptitiously seeing each other for a while. With a *y*," she said helpfully. "In the afternoons."

"And her address?"

"The next block," she said, pointing again. "Second on the left, with a black door."

"Any others at all?" Stone asked.

"Not that I am aware of," she replied.

Stone stood. "Thank you for your assistance, Mrs. Trask. I'm sorry to have intruded on your afternoon."

She shrugged. "Anything for the president," she said.

The Trask door closed behind them, and they got into the car.

"I know the way," Dino said, starting the car.

They found a parking place on the street, and as they were about to get out of the car, Stone pointed at the house with the window boxes. A well-dressed man carrying a briefcase was closing the door behind him and walking down the front steps. "Well, at least we won't have to deal with Mr. Brandon."

"How do we know that's Mr. Brandon?" Dino asked.

"You have a point."

They waited until the putative Mr. Brandon had cleared the block, then they walked to the house and rang the bell. Almost immediately, it was opened by a woman in a Chanel suit.

"Mrs. Brandon?" Stone said. "I am —"

"I know who you are," she said quickly. "Come inside before anyone sees you." She closed the door behind her. "Betty Trask called just now. You narrowly missed my husband, thank God! Come in here." She led the way to a cozy, paneled study, seated them, then closed the door. "Now," she said, perching on a small chair, "what do you want?"

"I'm sure Mrs. Trask told you why we're here," Stone said.

"Well, of course she did," Mrs. Brandon replied. "But what do you want from me? Brix Kendrick is dead and confessed in a letter, or so I read in the *Post*. A year has passed. Why are you dragging me into this?"

"Mrs. Brandon, you dragged yourself into this when you had an affair with Mr. Kendrick. We're simply investigating the circumstances of his and his wife's deaths, and we hope you can help us. This is not for publication."

"Oh, all right, what do you want?"

"How long were you and Mr. Kendrick, ah, seeing each other?"

"About two and a half months," she said.

"And where did you meet?"

"Here, in this house. Brix would leave the White House in the afternoons and come here for an hour or so. Do you want to know what we did?"

Stone ignored the question. "Do you know of anyone else Mr. Kendrick was seeing?"

"Milly Hart," she said. "She was before me. He admitted that to me."

"Were you jealous of Mrs. Hart?"

"Certainly not!" she said indignantly. "Why would I be jealous of that little tramp?"

"Are you aware that Milly Hart was having an affair with anyone besides Brixton Kendrick?"

She thought for a moment. "No," she murmured, aware that she had just called herself a tramp.

"Mrs. Brandon, what were your movements on the day Mrs. Kendrick died?"

"Am I a suspect? Am I under arrest? I want an attorney."

"Mrs. Brandon, you've been watching too much *Law & Order.* It's a simple question: where were you that day?"

"All day?"

"That would be helpful."

"I slept late, then I went to my monthly garden club luncheon."

"How long were you there?"

"From noon until around three. I was giving a presentation. After that, I had tea at a friend's house, and no, I will not tell you who that was, until we're in a courtroom."

"Did you see Mr. Kendrick at all that day?"

"No, I did not. The last time was the day before."

"How would you describe his frame of mind?" Stone asked.

"Serene. Brix was always serene. That's why I was surprised he killed himself."

"Why do you think he killed himself?"

"I should think it was obvious. He killed his own wife, for God's sake!"

"Did it surprise you when you heard of her death?"

"Of course it surprised me."

"Did you think Mr. Kendrick was the sort of man who would kill his wife?"

"Certainly not! Not for a moment."

"Did he ever say to you that he wanted out of his marriage?"

"No, never. He and Mimi were devoted to each other. He just had a very powerful sex drive."

Stone closed his notebook. "Thank you for seeing us, Mrs. Brandon," he said. "Can you tell me where Milly Hart lives?"

"Certainly not, I barely know the woman."

She led them to the door, and after looking both ways up and down the street, she let them out without a word and slammed the door behind them.

"Well, that was useful," Dino said.

"Sarcasm doesn't become you, Dino."

"What are we doing here?" Dino asked. "Every time somebody asks us what we want, I don't know what to tell them."

"Let's go find Milly Hart," Stone said.

20

Dino started the car. "Okay, tell me where Milly Hart lives."

"I don't know where she lives," Stone replied.

"Why do you think *I* know where she lives?"

Stone got out his cell phone and called Fair Sutherlin's direct line. Her secretary put him through.

"Good afternoon, Stone. Did you have a nice lunch with the president?"

"Very nice, thank you."

"You mean you *enjoyed* the food?"

"He gave us lobster salad," Stone said. "What's not to enjoy?"

"Wait until Kate hears about this."

"Oh, he had Kate's diet lunch, while Dino and I gorged ourselves."

"I see. I'm looking forward to seeing you tomorrow night. By the way, it's not black tie."

"I'm relieved to hear that, since I didn't bring a dinner jacket."

"What else can I do for you?" she asked, a leer in her voice.

"I've heard that the White House operators can find anybody."

"That is perfectly so."

"Would you kindly ask them to find the address of a woman named Milly Hart? With a *y?*"

"And who is Milly Hart with a *y?*"

"Someone Brixton Kendrick may have been having an affair with."

There was a dead silence, for a slow count of about four. "Brix Kendrick was having an *affair?*"

"At least one, maybe two."

"Good God! Who was the other one?"

"I'm going to tell you only because I know our reports cross your desk anyway. The other one, confirmed, is Muffy Brandon."

"Holy shit!" Fair said. "How do you know this?"

"It's Washington. Also, she admitted it to us ten minutes ago."

"Does the president know?"

"He knows of a rumor that Kendrick was having affairs. He doesn't know with whom yet, unless the grapevine in this town is even faster than I thought."

"It is," she said. "It moves faster than the speed of light, defying science."

"Then you should have Milly Hart's address in a millisecond," Stone said.

"Hang on," she said, and put him on hold.

"You making any progress?" Dino asked. "With the address, I mean?"

"I'll have it in a millisecond," Stone said.

Fair came back on the line. "She lives at the Watergate apartments. Who is she?"

"Didn't the White House operator fill you in?"

"I asked only for her address."

"Then you know just as much about her as I do," Stone said. "See you tomorrow night." He hung up. "She was flabbergasted to hear that Brix was having affairs," he said to Dino.

"I guess I'm the only guy in town who isn't," Dino said. "I always assume everybody is fucking everybody."

"That saves time," Stone said. "Can you find the Watergate apartments on the map?"

Dino consulted it. "Right by the Potomac River," he said. "I'm on my way." He put the car in gear.

"Then I'll come along for the ride."

Entrance to the apartment house required a stop at a reception desk.

"Milly Hart," Stone said to the uniformed doorman.

"Who shall I say is calling?"

"Mr. Stone Barrington and Lieutenant Dino Bacchetti."

The man wrote down the names, then dialed a number and spoke for a moment. He covered the receiver with his hand. "She doesn't know you," he said.

"May I speak with her?" Stone asked. The man handed him the phone. "Hello, Ms. Hart?"

"Yes?" It was a low voice, nice to listen to.

"This is Stone Barrington. I am here to speak to you at the request of the president of the United States."

"Really? Then give the phone to the doorman."

Stone did so, and the doorman gave him the apartment number and pointed him toward the elevators.

"We know nothing about this lady?" Dino said. "Nothing you haven't told me?"

"Zip, Dino."

"You sure about that?"

"Dino, you're sounding more like a wife at every turn."

The door opened directly into a handsome foyer, where a large arrangement of fresh flowers sat on an antique mahogany table.

"Very classy," Dino said.

A door opened, and a uniformed maid, their second of the day, beckoned them in. "This way, please."

Milly Hart simultaneously entered the living room through another door and walked toward them. She was a striking redhead wearing a negligee with a matching silk dressing gown, right out of an Arlene Dahl movie. In fact, she resembled Arlene Dahl in one of her old films. "Mr. Barrington? Lieutenant Bacchetti? How do you do?" she said, with an accent right off the New York stage. She extended a perfectly manicured hand and allowed both of them to shake it, then waved them to a sofa and took a chair. "You've piqued my curiosity with talk of the president," she said.

"We're speaking with you at his request."

"I'm flattered, but I've met the gentleman briefly only a few times, at White House dinners and such. What are you a lieutenant of?" she asked Dino. "I was expecting an army uniform."

"Of the New York City Police Department," Dino replied.

"Oh, dear," she said. "I hope this isn't about that parking ticket last winter. It was a hired car and driver, and I assumed his company would take care of it and bill me."

"No, ma'am," Dino said. "It's not about —"

"Would you gentlemen like some tea?" she asked. "It isn't too early, is it? Or would you prefer something more potent?"

"Tea would be lovely, Ms. Hart," Stone said.

"Please call me Milly," she said. "Absolutely everybody does."

"Thank you, Milly," Stone said. "I assure you the president has not taken an interest in your parking tickets."

"Oh, yes," she said. "Frankly, I thought you were making that up to get past the doorman."

"No, the president has asked us to look into the murder and apparent suicide of Emily and Brixton Kendrick."

For a moment, she nearly lost her composure, but she quickly recovered. "Really?"

"Really. We understand that you and Mr. Kendrick were . . . close."

"And where did you come by that particular item?"

"It's Washington," Dino said, looking pleased with himself.

"Ah, yes, so it is. Am I suspected of murdering one or both of them?"

"No, Milly," Stone said. "We're here because you and Brix Kendrick were having an affair."

"I remember the day the news broke," she said, ignoring his remark. "I was in New York at the time."

"You spend a lot of time in New York, do you?" Dino asked.

"I suppose I'm up there once a month, sometimes more often."

"We don't need an alibi from you," Stone said.

"Then, pray tell, what do you need?"

"We'd like to know who else Brix Kendrick was seeing."

"I'm sorry to disappoint you," she said, "but I am not privy to that information. Frankly, Brix did not seem to be the sort who would have affairs."

"And yet you were having an affair with him," Stone pointed out.

"I mean, multiple affairs," she replied. She still had not admitted her own affair, explicitly.

"What else can you tell us about Brix?" Stone asked.

"Gentlemen, I'm afraid I have nothing else to tell you." She looked at a diamond wristwatch adorning her slender wrist. "And I'm afraid I have forgotten another appointment for this hour. Will you gentlemen excuse me? I'm sorry about the tea."

She stood up, and the maid appeared as if on cue. "This way, gentlemen," she said.

Milly Hart turned and left the room without another word.

Stone and Dino found themselves in the entry hall, waiting for the elevator.

"I wonder what she's hiding," Stone said.

"You don't get it, do you?" Dino asked.

"Get what?"

"Milly Hart is a hooker."

21

They got into the elevator. "Why on earth do you think Milly Hart is a hooker?" Stone asked.

"Stone, sometimes you are so fucking naive."

"What?"

"We go to see a woman without an appointment. She walks in clad in Hollywood lingerie, then, while we are questioning her, she suddenly remembers another appointment."

The elevator doors opened, and, standing before them was Muffy Brandon's husband. They got off, and he got on.

"Are you getting the picture now?" Dino asked.

"I believe so," Stone said. "I'm sorry to be so slow on the uptake."

"The question is, how did Brixton Kendrick afford a high-priced hooker like Milly Hart? He was a government employee, for

God's sake."

"Private income?" Stone asked.

"Not according to his son. Remember meeting him?"

"Ah, yes, and he was terribly concerned about getting the max out of selling the old man's house."

"And we've gotta be talking about at least a grand a pop for an hour of Milly Hart's time."

"I don't have any experience with rates for hookers," Stone said.

"Well, you've gotta admit that Milly is a rare beauty, especially in a town full of women like Betty Trask and Muffy Brandon."

"I can't argue with that. I don't suppose Brix Kendrick would have any trouble wanting her. Except that his days already seemed pretty full."

"Yeah," Dino said, "he must have been short of time with Muffy waiting for him in the afternoons, and he couldn't have been seeing somebody else in the evenings, because he was busy being an ideal husband. The question is, how could he get it up that often, at his age?"

"How old was he?" Stone asked.

"According to the FBI report, both he and Mimi were fifty-one, the age at which half of American men have what is politely called 'erectile dysfunction.' "

"Well, Brix was obviously not having those problems, because he was keeping at least two ladies happy on a regular basis."

"Maybe his wife had cut him off, for one reason or another," Dino suggested. "And believe me, they don't really need a reason."

"Horniness is not a motive for murder, especially when he couldn't possibly have been horny."

"Shame is a motive for suicide, though," Dino pointed out.

"I guess," Stone said.

They got into the car.

"Where to?" Dino asked.

"Home, James. We've got nobody else to talk to, except each other."

Teddy Fay and Lauren Cade finished cleaning their hangar apartment and got into a shower together.

"You know," she said, soaping Teddy's back, "this place isn't half bad."

"Have I ever asked you to live in a place that *was* half bad?"

"No, you've done very well by me in that regard. Tell me, what are we going to do with ourselves in D.C.?"

"Well," Teddy said, starting to soap her

front, "I've got some work to do on a couple of gadgets." Teddy had made a fortune inventing kitchen tools that were sold on late-night television. "Gotta keep the money tap running."

"I won't argue with you about that," Lauren said. "I want to see the National Gallery and the Smithsonian. I've never been to Washington before."

"There are enough museums and galleries to keep you busy for a year," Teddy said. "Not that I think we'll be here for a year. I know you get antsy if you're too far from a beach for too long. I just want to be here long enough to throw Todd Bacon and his crew off the track."

Todd Bacon, at that moment, was in San Diego fielding phone calls from his team, and he was baffled by the result. They had found three instances of Cessna 182 RG landings at West Coast general aviation airports, but each of them had been traced to owners who were obviously not Teddy Fay.

"You look puzzled," his number two said.

"Aren't you? Where the hell did he go?"

"Well, if he isn't on the West Coast, that leaves forty-five other states where he could have landed. Oh, and did I mention

Canada?"

"Don't be a smart-ass," Todd said.

"Todd, if we don't get a solid lead soon, they're gonna pull the plug on us," number two said. "We're going to find ourselves in some South American jungle looking for drug factories, and I don't like bugs and snakes."

"I'm thinking," Todd said, "I'm thinking."

22

Stone, Dino, and Shelley turned up at Fair Sutherlin's place fashionably late; they were the first ones there. Fair lived in a small, elegant apartment building on a broad avenue near Dupont Circle, and her space, its furnishings and pictures indicated an income of which her government salary was but a small part.

As Dino was introducing Shelley, two other couples arrived, and before those introductions had been made there were six couples present, including a network anchorman, a columnist for the *Washington Post,* and a right-wing Republican senator, each with a wife in tow. Everybody was terribly glad to see everybody else.

A young man in a white jacket took drink orders, and a young woman in a white jacket poured champagne for those who did not have another choice. They drank for forty minutes, then someone opened a pair of sliding doors, and the twelve took seats around a long, beautifully set table.

"Fair," the senator's wife said, "I don't know how you have amassed so many beautiful things in your short life."

"By the deaths of my parents and all four of my grandparents," Fair replied. "I'm an only child, and I have three very complete sets of china, silver, and crystal, in opposing patterns. By the way, since Stone, Dino, and Shelley are new at my table, I should tell them about my one rule: no politics will be discussed."

There were murmurs of assent, then there was complete silence for a little more than a minute.

"How 'bout those Redskins," the anchorman offered.

"Not until next month," Fair said.

The senator spoke up. "Stone, Dino, tell us about how your investigation is going."

"First of all, Senator," Stone said, "I am not shocked that you know about our investigation. Second, as you must know, we can't discuss it before we have made our final report to the president, and maybe not even then."

The columnist gave a snort. "I would imagine that the collective knowledge about your investigation by those present at this table amounts to very nearly everything you have learned so far. For instance, I hear that you had a conversation with the notorious Milly Hart yesterday."

"I can neither confirm nor deny that," Stone said, "but I would be interested to know why she is notorious."

"Because she's a high-priced hooker," Dino said.

The table made an affirmative noise.

"What is Ms. Hart's story?" Stone asked the columnist.

"Well, let's see if I can encapsulate it in one short paragraph," the man said. "Well-brought-up girl comes to Washington and works for an important senator, one Gerald Hart, of Virginia; marries senator; senator dies, leaving a widow surprised that he left her so little; senator's federal pension is insufficient to keep widow in style to which she has become accustomed; then someone offers her funds to tide her over, affection presumed; then someone else offers, and pretty soon widow is living stylishly again."

"I hear Milly has a stylish clientele, too," the anchorman's wife said.

"Was Brix Kendrick among them?" the columnist's wife asked, directing her question to Stone.

"You tell us," Stone said, "please. We're

new in town."

"Frankly," said the anchorman, "I don't know how Brix could afford her, on his White House salary."

The senator grinned. "Perhaps someone should audit Brix's books at the White House," he said, pointing his fork at Fair. "After all, he reigned over a considerable budget. My committee has seen the numbers."

"Senator," Fair said, "the audit has already been done, and everything was in apple-pie order."

"Apple pie can be messy," the senator replied.

"Not *our* apple pie," Fair said.

"Oh, that's right," the senator said. "Will Lee is notoriously proper about budgets."

"And notoriously transparent, too," Fair responded.

"No skeletons in that closet, then," the senator admitted.

"Well," said the columnist, "not the budgetary closet, anyway. There are, of course, other closets, and upright, dull Brix was, apparently, occupying a crowded one."

That got a laugh from the table.

"I should think," the senator's wife said, "that that would make Brix neither upright nor dull. I can't imagine how a man of his age could manage so well." She shot a meaningful glance at her husband across the table, and he looked uncomfortable.

"Someone has pointed out to me," Stone said, "that, at fifty-one, Brix's age, half of American males are experiencing erectile dysfunction. Has it occurred to anyone that Brix might be among the other half? Or perhaps among an even smaller percentage who are raging bulls at that age?"

"Hugh Hefner is in his eighties," Fair said, "and he seems to be holding up well."

The senator snorted. "All that guy has to do is lie still," he said, "and they do it for him."

The anchorman laughed. "I hope I can lie that still when I'm his age."

"I hope so, too, dear," his wife said.

Shelley spoke up. "Would anyone care to hazard a guess as to who else is on Milly Hart's preferred list?"

"At least one senator, I hear," the columnist said, raising his eyebrows in the direction of the senator present.

"I wouldn't know about that," the senator said. "And even if I did, senate cloakroom gossip is privileged."

"Only if we can't pry it out of you," Fair said.

Everybody laughed.

"He's apparently right," his wife said. "He won't even tell *me* what's said in that cloakroom."

"I recall," the columnist said, "that Warren G. Harding, when he was a senator, is alleged to have impregnated a young woman on a sofa in that cloakroom."

"That the young woman was impregnated by Warren G. is not in doubt, though the geography in question is a little hazy. I think that information," the senator said, "was traced to the young woman herself, though she may have embroidered her story for effect. It did not come from one of Senator Harding's colleagues, though."

Everyone moved back to the living room for coffee, and Stone asked Fair for the powder room.

"I believe it's occupied," Fair said, "but use my bathroom." She pointed to a door.

Stone opened it and found himself in a very feminine bedroom. He crossed it and found the bath, and while he stood at the toilet, he could not keep himself from opening the medicine chest on the wall before his nose. He found prescription bottles for a painkiller, a sleeping pill, and a couple he did not recognize.

Also, he was intrigued to find a clear plastic case containing four lipsticks, the same brand that he had been told about by Shelley, apparently part of a promotion, none of which was Pagan Spring. There was, however, an empty space in the case. One lipstick had been removed.

He stopped by her dressing table on his way back to the living room, but found no Pagan Spring there, either. He was, he reflected, going to have to make a trip to a drugstore.

23

Teddy Fay had finished bringing his hangar apartment up to his standard of living, and now he sat at his work table, putting the final touches on a peeler/slicer combination for his usual client. He prepared it for sending to a mail drop in Missouri that would, in turn, forward it to the addressee. In due course, if his client found it acceptable, and Teddy was certain he would, funds would be wired to a numbered account in the Cayman Islands, making Teddy awash in cash. Royalties from later sales would keep the stream flowing.

Bored with the fine work, he turned his thoughts elsewhere, and a whim struck him. He donned a fresh pair of latex gloves and opened a packet of very common stationery, sold in many drugstores, then uncapped his silver Montblanc pen.

My dear Miss Holly Barker: It has

been some time since we last communicated, and longer still since we actually met, and I felt I should express a few thoughts to you.

I am aware that you have risen quickly in the estimation of your colleagues at the Agency and that with the rather self-serving help of Lance Cabot, the ultimate careerist, and the approbation of Director Katharine Rule Lee, you have moved up in the Agency's structure with considerable speed. I am aware, too, that you have been assigned, from time to time, to supervise operations. This, again, is self-serving on Lance's part, since it is important to him to have an assistant deputy director with actual experience with running agents.

However, there is beginning to appear a blot on your copybook, as it were, and you must take steps to correct that, if you do not wish your progress up the ladder to be impeded in committee. I refer, as you may have supposed, to the assignment of young Todd Bacon to his current task, and to his repeated failures to complete it successfully.

Young Todd is, in many respects, the ideal officer. He is a planner, meticulous and thorough, and can even be inventive. He lacks, however, the most important qualities of the best operatives: imagination and the ability to improvise on the move. Like a mediocre chess player, he thinks only of the next move and not the two or three down the road.

That having been said, the Agency has always needed people like Todd Bacon to do the planning and dogwork that every operation requires, without actually serving at the pointed end of the mission, where dash and quick thinking are required for success. It occurs to me that young Todd is very nearly at the point where it would be difficult if not impossible to move him sideways into a position where he could contribute on a consistent basis and earn himself some praise and, eventually, a pension.

I know, of course, that his current assignment is off the books and, thus, not subject to the usual committee scrutiny that accompanies most operations, but that very fact puts you, and to a lesser extent Lance, in the hot seat. Lance, to the lesser extent, because if there should be heat to be taken, he will arrange for you to take it.

So, it is time for one of two things to happen: either close the books on Todd's mission and reassign him (it occurs to me that the boy might eventually do well in my old department, Technical Services — he is, after all, proficient with computers, weapons, and the like), or, the other thing: assign someone with both the professional and personal qualities to make a success of the mission.

However, there are thorns in those rosebushes, too. First, it would be difficult to transfer a successful officer from sanctioned missions to an off-the-books one without stunting his career or, perhaps, making a larger number of Agency people aware of what he is doing. And even should he be successful, no one will ever know about it but you, Lance, and the director, at least until that officer gets around to publishing his memoirs in Sweden or writing a roman à clef. Nor will it do you much good with the director, since she will, along with her estimable husband, be on her way in eighteen months or so.

Lance, it is clear, longs to replace the director with himself, with the resulting elevation of yourself to the highest realms of the Agency and the government. He may well think it is not the time to indulge in off-the-books missions.

And as for you, there is only one person you could appoint to replace young Todd, someone with the wit and the moxie to pull it off, and that is your own sweet self. You have already had one very good shot at pulling it off, of course, but that was, at best, a near miss, and one does not build a career at the top on a structure of near misses.

I hope you are able to make or at least influence the right decision. I am living quietly, now, with no great wish to be a bother to anyone, but as you might imagine, if my nest is disturbed, I might be annoyed enough to sting again. I am fond of you, in my way, and I hope you will not be the one to receive the stinger.

Should you and Lance wish to put an end to all this, please insert a small display advertisement in the Arts section of the National Edition of the New York Times on the last day of this month, to read: NANCY, ALL IS WELL, CALL HOME.

Should the ad not appear, I shall assume that peace is not possible, and shall resume making a nuisance of myself.

With kind thoughts,

T.

■ ■ ■ ■

Holly Barker slit open the plain white envelope with no return address. It would have already been subjected to X-ray and chemical analysis before reaching her desk, so she did not fear it. She read through the letter once, not stopping to analyze what was written, then she folded it, returned it to its envelope, and walked to the door that separated her office from Lance's suite. She rapped on the door, sharply, twice.

"Come in, Holly," Lance responded.

She opened the door and entered.

"And have a seat," Lance said.

Holly handed him the envelope.

"Something to brighten my day, I hope," Lance said. He seemed in a good mood. "What is your take on whatever this is?"

"I have no take," Holly said. "No point of view, no recommendation. Nothing."

Lance peered at her over his reading glasses. "That is very unlike you," he said.

"The letter presents the situation as well, or better, than I could. It is not particularly flattering to either of us, and it is, of course, self-serving of the writer, but you have to see its contents. Go ahead, read it."

"Right now? It's a busy morning."

She wanted to see his face when he read it. "I think right now would be the best time."

"So it's time-sensitive?"

"Read the fucking letter, Lance," she said, as evenly as she could.

Lance gave her a long look, then turned his attention to the letter. He read it slowly and occasionally winced or glowered or lifted his eyebrows. He finished it and laid it on his desk. "Has this been processed?"

"It has had the usual scrutiny inbound; it did not appear to have been opened."

"Have you taken any steps to process it further?"

Holly shook her head slowly. "No. Process it, if you like, but I can recite the report now." She looked at the wall above Lance's head. " 'This document has been processed to the fullest extent by this department. It is written by hand, in felt-tip ink, on widely available twenty-five-percent cotton paper and presents no fingerprints, fibers, DNA, or any other evidence that would profit from further analysis.' In short, it's clean."

Lance leaned back in his chair, rested his feet on his desk, and ruminated for a moment. "I am having lunch — let's see, the day after tomorrow — with the director of Technical Services. I will suggest to him that

I have a well-qualified officer in my bailiwick who cannot be promoted further, and that it is my belief that he would make a fine addition to the Tech Services team. If that doesn't work, I'll speak to someone in analysis, and if that doesn't work, you will reassign Mr. Bacon to a subordinate position at a station in an uncomfortable climate, remote from suitable women or other entertainment."

"I understand. And then what?"

"Would you be willing to replace Bacon on his current assignment?"

"I would not," Holly replied. "Not under threat of transfer, of discharge, or of death. I would rather eat my gun than pursue this any further." Lance began to speak, but Holly held up a hand. "And let me say this, before saying nothing further: his allusion to the hornets' nest is a threat, and not an idle one, and I do not think now is the time to provoke him."

Lance returned his feet to the floor and the letter to Holly. "All right, shred this and put the paper in a burn bag. Recall Mr. Bacon and his team for reassignment, and see that each of them is individually debriefed in such a way that he would not dream of speaking to anyone, even in his prayers, of his past duty with regard to this person.

"When Mr. Bacon returns to this office I will see him, if I have been able to procure for him a decent reassignment. If not, you will throw your body across my office door, see him in my stead, and give him his new assignment and a month's paid leave during which to contemplate his future with the Agency. Also, place the ad in the *Times.* Is there anything else?"

"Shall I notify the director?"

"You shall not. I shall do that at an appropriate time. Good day."

"Good day, Lance," Holly said, rising and returning to her office. Her forehead was damp, as were her armpits and her crotch, but she felt the relief of having dodged a hellfire missile aimed at her head.

24

Holly placed the ad in the *Times,* then composed an e-mail to Todd Bacon at an e-mail address that required a ten-digit password to access. "Call off your party immediately, as the guest of honor is permanently unavailable. You and the kids come home and see me at seven A.M. Friday. Bring your own breakfast. Barker."

She looked at Teddy's letter for a long minute, then disobeyed orders: she made a copy and put the original in her briefcase, then she shredded the copy, emptied the shredder into a burn bag, and gave it to her secretary for disposal. She was determined that this was not going to come back and bite her on the ass.

Todd Bacon, still on the West Coast, opened the e-mail on rising and read it. "Shit!" he shouted, waking up the man in the other bed.

"What?" the man yelled back.

"It's over, goddammit. They've pulled the plug. Call everybody now and tell them we're due at Langley Friday A.M., first thing."

"Worst fears realized," the man said.

"Maybe not," Todd said. "I'm not dead yet."

On the appointed day, Teddy drove to a little bookstore in D.C. that stocked the New York, Washington, and National editions of the *Times,* bought a paper, then went back to his car and opened the Arts section. His tight face spread into a grin. The ad was there.

He drove slowly home and found Lauren making breakfast. "I think it may be over," he said.

"Your letter worked?" she asked, incredulous.

Teddy handed her the newspaper, folded back to the ad.

"I don't believe it," she said.

"Neither do I," he replied, "at least not yet. We'll give it a while, and if we have no further problems, we'll pick us a spot and go live happily ever after."

"And if we have further problems?"

Teddy sighed. "We'll burn that bridge when we come to it."

■ ■ ■ ■

Stone was still working on the *Times* crossword when the phone rang. "Hello?"

"Mr. Barrington?" A woman's voice, silken.

"Yes?"

"This is Milly Hart."

"Good morning, Ms. Hart," he said.

"I would be pleased if you would come to lunch today at my apartment, if you're available."

"May I bring my colleague?"

"I would prefer to see you alone."

"I'm available."

"One o'clock, then?"

"One o'clock." Stone hung up, got out of bed, and went into the living room, where Dino was reading the *Wall Street Journal.* Dino had become interested in financial matters after the multimillion-dollar divorce settlement arranged by his former father-in-law, Eduardo Bianchi.

"Who was on the phone?" Dino asked.

"Milly Hart."

Dino looked surprised. "Yeah? That sounds interesting."

"That remains to be seen," Stone replied. "She invited me to lunch."

"Just you?"
"I asked if I could bring you — she said no."
Dino smiled. "She's going to jump your bones."
"I doubt it," Stone said, "but I think she may have something to say. I wanted you to know up front that it wasn't my idea to see her alone, it was hers."
"It's okay, pal," Dino said.
"You sure about that?"
"I'm sure. Anyway, there's a movie on HBO I want to see."
"Okay," Stone said.

Stone presented himself at the Watergate apartments at five minutes past the hour, and the maid was waiting for him when he got off the elevator. She showed him into the living room, where Milly Hart was sitting on the sofa, just as last time, in another beautiful peignoir. She offered him a hand and patted the sofa next to her. "Thank you for coming, Mr. Barrington," she said.
"I never turn down a free lunch," Stone replied, sitting.
"Marilyn," she said to the maid, "you may have the afternoon off."
"Yes, ma'am," the woman said, smiling. She disappeared.

As soon as she left, there was a knock on the door from the foyer.

"Come in," Milly called out.

The door opened, and a waiter pushed in a room service table and set it up before the windows overlooking the river.

"Come," Milly said, leading Stone to the table. "I believe you're fond of lobster salad," she said, waving him to his seat.

"You're very well informed," Stone said, surprised.

"It's Washington," she said.

Stone laughed. "I was surprised to hear from you."

"I'm sorry I had to cut our first meeting short, but you hadn't called ahead, and I had another engagement."

"I believe I bumped into your engagement as we got off the elevator."

"Did you," she said, but it wasn't a question. She poured them each a glass of a good white Burgundy, and they raised their glasses. "To truth and justice and the American way," she said.

Stone smiled and sipped his wine.

"I take those things very seriously," she said, popping a morsel of lobster into her mouth.

"Is that how you were brought up?"

"Well, yes, but it was my late husband,

Senator Hart, who instilled those values in me in a more permanent way. Since he died, I have hated injustice in its every form, and I always tell the truth."

"Are you going to tell me the truth today?" Stone asked.

"I am, to the extent that I know it." She sipped her wine. "Tell me, what have you heard about me?"

"That you come from good stock, that you married a good man, but one who left you in dire straits."

She smiled broadly. "And that I was forced to take money from men as a result?"

"Something like that."

"I'm afraid the truth is more shocking than that," she said.

"I can't wait to hear it," Stone said.

So she told him.

25

"Only some of what you have heard is true," Milly Hart said. "I did come from good stock. I am well educated, hold a master's degree in English literature from Mount Holyoke College. I did marry a good man, and he did die sooner than I would have wished, but he did not leave me in dire straits."

"I'm glad to hear that," Stone said.

"He left me quite well off, in fact: a little more than six million in securities, two small office buildings that produce a very good income, an apartment in New York, and a house in Virginia. And in the ensuing years I have improved my positions in almost everything, thanks to good advice from good friends."

She took a sip of her wine. "And," she said, "I have never taken a penny from a man for sex."

Stone didn't know what to say.

"I do have . . . relationships," she said, "and quite often more than one at a time. You see, when I married the senator we formed a tight physical bond and we enjoyed a *very* active sex life, so much so that, when he died, I found myself sharply wanting that to continue." She took another sip.

"Please go on," Stone said.

"The most difficult thing was that I was suddenly a widow and expected not to form attachments with men for quite some time. Fortunately, someone came to the rescue: a married man."

"I see," Stone said, though he didn't quite.

"I couldn't be seen out with men, and of course he couldn't be seen out with women, so we met here and . . . at other places." She polished off the last of her lobster and took a gulp of wine. "His name was Brixton Kendrick."

Stone scooped up the last of his lobster and kept his mouth shut.

"Brix understood me, and he knew that because of his marriage and his work, he could not offer me the kind of attention I required — that is, *enough* attention. So he suggested I take other married lovers. He even suggested one or two."

Stone sipped his wine, entranced.

"The gentleman you encountered when

you got off the elevator yesterday is one of them, and one of the nicest. We see each other once a week, always varying the day, and we enjoy ourselves."

"I don't know how many there are," Stone said, "but they are very fortunate men."

She colored slightly. "That's very kind of you, Stone," she said.

"Kindness has nothing to do with it," Stone said. "You are a very beautiful woman."

"Thank you," she breathed. "I am aware of your situation," she said. "In fact, I knew and liked Arrington. My Virginia home is not far from the house she built. I was invited to her housewarming on that day, but I had other plans in New York and had to send my regrets. That was a terrible day for you, I know, and I understand how you must have been feeling during the months since that time."

"Thank you," Stone said.

"I find you a very attractive man," she said, standing. Her peignoir had fallen open, and her body was exposed its whole length.

She was a real redhead, Stone noted. He slipped an arm around her waist and kissed her, and the peignoir fell to the floor.

"Come," she said, taking his hand and leading him into her bedroom, a large sunny place with a bed that was already turned down. She did not bother to close the curtains, she simply lay on the bed and watched him, smiling, as he undressed.

In his arms she was luscious and ready, and she welcomed him with all her charms.

An hour later, both of them spent, they lay beside each other. Then she got out of bed, left the room, and returned, still naked, with half a bottle of champagne and two crystal flutes. They piled up the pillows and sat back, sipping the cold wine.

"And now," she said, "having had carnal knowledge of you, I will tell you why else I asked you here. I meant to tell you sooner, but I was overcome."

"Tell me," Stone said.

"I was not Brix's only lover," she said.

"I heard that he was seeing Muffy Brandon. I spoke to her."

"Oh, not Muffy," she said. "I mean, yes, he was fucking her, but I also mean he was seeing someone much more important to him."

"Brix was quite a guy," Stone said.

"Someone in the White House," Milly said quietly.

Stone nearly choked on his champagne.

"You see, in his position, Brix had the run

of the place, saw everyone, knew everyone, knew when he could take a quiet moment, lock a door, and conduct an assignation."

"In the White House?" Stone asked, flabbergasted.

"Oh, yes. For Brix, knowing what he knew about that world, there was no safer place."

"I'm having some difficulty accepting this."

"I'm telling you only what Brix told me. It wasn't always in the White House, he said. After all, Mimi worked, and he did have his own house. There is a garage, and someone could drive right in and enter the house unseen."

"How very convenient," Stone said.

"On other occasions they used the White House family quarters."

Stone sat up in bed and faced her. "Are you telling me he was having an affair with . . ."

"With Katharine Rule Lee? Possibly, he wouldn't say. But the family quarters were sometimes available when the president was traveling, or just in the daytime, and Brix had full access, keys and everything. I mean, not in the presidential bed, but there are a number of bedrooms in the quarters, and they are usually unused. Brix knew the schedules of the cleaners, and the Secret

Service wouldn't enter the quarters without his permission. I think that the apparent impossibility of what he was doing was a big thrill for him."

"I can see how it could be," Stone said. "As far as you know, did anyone at the White House suspect?"

"He told me once that there was someone who had seemed to know something, but he couldn't be sure. So he just continued as he had before."

"Did he mention a name?"

"No, Brix was a very discreet man."

"Did Mimi know about these other women?"

"I think she preferred not to know. If Mimi had been a more attentive and adventurous wife, none of this would ever have happened. I think she viewed sex, perhaps for religious reasons, as a means of procreation and little else. He told me once that she was shocked when he tried to give her cunnilingus, and disgusted by the thought of giving him fellatio. She wouldn't touch his cock with her hand." She glanced at the bedside clock.

"Perhaps I'd better go," Stone said.

"I do have an appointment at five o'clock, and God knows, after what we've been doing, I need a nap."

Stone got into his clothes, and she walked him to the elevator, still nude. "I'm in New York once, sometimes twice a month," she said. "I have an apartment at the Carlyle Hotel. Would you like to see me there sometime?"

"I would be delighted," Stone said. He gave her his card.

"No attachments, no entanglements. I prefer it that way," she said.

"I understand. That's fine with me."

They kissed, then he got onto the elevator. His last image of her was her standing, naked and relaxed, blowing him a kiss.

"Dino is not going to believe this," Stone said aloud to himself. "Not any of it."

26

Stone found Dino watching a ball game in the living room of their suite. "Who's winning?" he asked, not that he cared. Stone was not a big sports fan.

"The Yankees, of course," Dino said.

"You want to wait until it's over before I tell you what happened?"

Dino muted the TV. "You ended up in the sack with her, didn't you?"

"I don't like your accusatory tone," Stone said, "and a gentleman would never answer that question."

"You just did," Dino said.

"Never mind that. Milly had a lot to say, and I think you'll find it interesting."

"There was time for talking?" Dino asked "You're losing your touch."

"You want to hear this, or you want to watch the fucking ball game?"

Dino switched off the TV. "All right, I'm all ears."

"First of all, she didn't fall on hard times after her husband's death — quite the contrary. And she doesn't take money from men."

"And you bought it?"

"She has a list of lovers, all or most of them married, but she's not a hooker — she just likes sex."

"She told you that?"

"No names, except the guy we saw yesterday, and of course Brix Kendrick. He was her first lover after her husband died."

"Did anything she say have anything to do with why we're here, or are we just gossiping?"

"Dino, she says that Brix told her he had a lover in the White House."

"Anybody we know?"

"He wouldn't give her the name, but they were doing it in the White House."

"That's impossible."

Stone explained why it wasn't.

"And you think it's the first lady?"

"No, of course not, even though Milly said that was a possibility."

"Why don't we go back to New York and let Milly solve this?" Dino asked.

"You're not paying attention, Dino. Now we have a motive for the murder."

"I must have missed that."

"Jealousy. Brix's lover was jealous of his wife, or she wanted her out of the way so she'd have a clear shot at Brix."

"Sounds like she had already hit the bull's-eye," Dino pointed out.

"The bull's-eye was to have Brix all to herself."

"I can't say I like your theory all that much."

"Have you got a better one? Have you got a theory at all?"

"Yeah, I think Brix had a scene with his wife, offed her, then, out of remorse, offed himself."

"No," Stone said, "Brix left ahead of Mimi — they were in separate cars, remember, and when he heard she was dead he knew who had done it. His remorse was that his affair led to his wife's death."

"Why do you always like the complicated motives?" Dino asked. "What's wrong with simple?"

"This is just one step removed from simple," Stone said. "His lover saw Mimi leave the tennis court. Maybe there was a confrontation, words were exchanged, names called. Mimi turned to leave, and the lover grabbed the first thing handy — the brick — and hit her with it or threw it at her."

"Having first paused to kiss the brick, leaving her Pagan Spring lipstick on it," Dino said. "I like that part."

"All right, I don't know how the lipstick got on the brick," Stone admitted. "I'll give you that one."

"Thanks, I feel so much better."

"Oh, come on, you know this scenario works."

"So tell me, how are we better off than before you and Milly did the deed?"

"We're better off because we know who to talk to now," Stone replied.

"We do? I missed another one."

"The maids who clean the family quarters."

"You're saying Brix was using the family quarters to fuck his girlfriend?"

"I explained that, being in charge of the house, he had all the keys, and he knew the maids' cleaning schedule."

"Oh, yeah, I forgot about that."

"Look, Dino, our backs are against the wall here. We can either send the president and first lady a nice note accepting the FBI report and go home, or we can run down this lead. What's it going to be?"

"I think 'lead' is too strong a term," Dino said, "but what the hell? You talk to the maids, I'll listen. *Then* we'll write the Lees a nice note and go home."

"Okay, I'll set it up with the White House," Stone said. "And, Dino, you cannot roll over in bed and tell Shelley about it. She has a vested interest in protecting the FBI in all this and she could screw it up for us."

"You think she'd do that?" Dino asked.

"Inadvertently, maybe, but she might mention it to Kerry Smith, and that would not be good."

"What about you, pal? You going to roll over in bed and tell Holly about this?"

"We're working for Holly, sort of," Stone pointed out. "God knows, we've had little else to tell her."

"You seeing her tonight?"

"Yes. Here."

"Then lock your door. I'm seeing Shelley here, too."

"Will do."

"Gee, I hope you won't be all worn out after your matinee," Dino said.

"You have a point. It's been a while since I've had a matinee."

"Well, I'm glad you're back in the game," Dino said. He clicked on the TV. "And so am I."

The phone rang, and Stone answered it. He listened for a moment. "All right," he said, "send them up." He put down the phone.

"Send who up?" Dino asked.

"The front desk said there are two D.C. cops downstairs."

The doorbell rang, and Stone let in two men he could have spotted as cops from half a mile.

"I'm Paulson," one of them said, "this is Padgett." He nodded toward his partner. "Are you Barrington?"

"I am," Stone said. "Nice to meet you, gentlemen. That's Lieutenant Bacchetti, NYPD, over there, glued to the ball game."

Dino gave them a little wave.

Stone led them to a sofa. "What's up?"

The two men sat down. "Well," Paulson said, consulting his notebook, "the head doorman at the Watergate apartments tells us that you paid a Mrs. Hart a visit this afternoon."

"I had lunch with her," Stone said.

"And what time did you leave her apartment?"

"Around four."

"Then maybe you can tell us how the lady got dead."

27

Stone stared at the cop. "What are you talking about?"

"And you were the last person to see her alive," the cop said.

"Tell me what has happened before you ask me another question," Stone said.

The cop consulted his notebook. "A gentleman named Brandon arrived at the Watergate apartments at five P.M., and the doorman, as instructed by Ms. Hart, sent him straight up. No phone call was made. Mr. Brandon arrived on her floor, and when the elevator doors opened, he found Ms. Hart lying in the vestibule, wearing some sort of negligee, dead."

"How was she killed?" Stone asked.

"It's too soon for the ME's report," the cop said, "but from the looks of her, she was bludgeoned to death with a blunt instrument."

"Time of death?"

"We don't have that yet, but it happened sometime between when you arrived for lunch, a little after one P.M., and when Mr. Brandon arrived at five."

Stone looked at his watch. "It's five forty-five. How'd you get here so fast?"

"There's a captain, a lieutenant, four detectives, and a crime-scene team on the spot. They didn't need us, so we were sent over here as soon as we arrived."

"How'd you know where to find me?"

"Are you kidding?" the cop asked. "Everybody in town knows about you two."

"Yeah, I know," Stone said. "It's Washington."

"Right."

"All right, then," Stone said, "I left at four. She died sometime between then and five. You've got a better window."

"We've got a better window, if we buy your story."

"He got here at four-fifteen," Dino said. "I'm your witness, and the hotel staff can put me here since breakfast."

The two cops looked at each other. "Okay," Paulson said, "she died between four and five."

"I take it there was a lot of blood," Stone said. "Was it clotting yet?"

"It was slippery," Paulson replied.

"Then closer to five than four."

"Makes sense," Paulson said. "The woman was wearing a negligee with a kind of robe over it."

"It's called a peignoir," Stone said, then spelled it for him.

Paulson wrote it down. "Okay, if you say so. Is that what she was wearing when you last saw her?"

Stone took a breath to answer, then stopped.

"Let me make it easier for you," Paulson said. "There'll be a rape kit."

"All right," Stone said, "she was naked when I last saw her. She walked me to the elevator."

Paulson made a note.

"But your rape kit won't show anything from me, she was too fastidious a person. The fact that she was wearing the peignoir is an indication that she bathed or showered, then got dressed."

"And why do you think she was fastidious?" Paulson asked.

"You'll have to take my word for it," Stone said.

"The word around town is that the lady has been receiving paying guests for some time," Padgett said, speaking for the first time.

"I think that when you investigate further, you'll find that the rumors about that are untrue, that she doesn't need funds from men. She did tell me she had had a number of lovers since her husband's death, and I knew about Brandon."

"She tell you about him?"

"Dino and I left there yesterday, just as Brandon arrived."

"That's true," Dino said.

"You know Brandon, do you?"

"Only by sight," Stone said. "We spoke with his wife yesterday at their home, as part of our investigation. We saw him leave the house just before we arrived. Ms. Hart told me she had a weekly appointment with him, always on a different day."

"So Brandon saw her both yesterday and today?" Padgett asked.

"So it seems."

"That doesn't sound like weekly to me."

"No, it doesn't. She didn't explain the extra visit this week. I have to tell you, fellas, Brandon sounds like a better fit for this than me."

"Maybe," Padgett said, "but why would he see her weekly for months, then get off the elevator one day, bludgeon her to death, then call us?"

"He made the call?"

"From his cell phone. He waited for us in the lobby."

"Then maybe he isn't such a good fit," Stone said.

"You got any other theories about who might have done this?" Padgett asked. "Anything she said to you . . . at lunch give you any clues?"

Stone shook his head. "Nobody comes to mind from what she said. I don't have a name for you."

"You think this killing might somehow be related to your investigation?" Padgett asked.

"I don't have any evidence to support that theory."

"All right," Padgett said, and the two cops stood up. He handed Stone a card. "If you think of anything, you know the drill."

"I do," Stone said. "And I'll call." He showed the cops out.

"Well," Dino said, "you didn't actually lie to them."

"No, I didn't."

"But you do think the killing is related to our investigation?"

"I have that hunch," Stone said. "I think somebody thought Milly might tell us something and wanted to shut her up. But, as I told the cops, I don't have any evidence to support that."

"You don't have any evidence to support *anything,*" Dino said.

"Don't rub it in."

"Well, if it's any consolation, I think your hunch is right, and I think your theory about a lover inside the White House is looking better, too."

"Thank you, Dino."

"Why don't you make that call and set up the meeting with the maids who clean the family quarters?"

Stone picked up the phone and called Fair Sutherlin's direct line.

"Ms. Sutherlin's office, this is Charlotte Kirby," a woman said.

"This is Stone Barrington, Ms. Kirby. Is Ms. Sutherlin available?"

"She's got somebody in there at the moment," the secretary said.

"Would you tell her that I'd be grateful if she would set up a meeting with the staff who clean the president's family quarters?"

"Certainly, I will."

"Tomorrow, perhaps?"

"I'll tell her that, and I'll probably be the one setting up the meeting. May I reach you at the Hay-Adams, Mr. Barrington?"

"Yes. And thank you, Ms. Kirby."

"You're very welcome, Mr. Barrington." She hung up.

28

Todd Bacon and his team met, by previous arrangement, in the parking lot at Langley, all seven of them.

"What's going on, Todd?" his number two asked.

"I don't know, and that's the truth. What I suspect is that we're being shut down and transferred. Certainly, there's no reason to think we might be jettisoned. When the day is over, call my cell and leave a message. All I want from you is one of four words: one, 'excellent' means you got a better assignment; two, 'satisfactory' means it was a sideways move but acceptable; three, 'unsatisfactory' means a demotion but you're still working here; four, 'unacceptable' means you got the ax or quit. I'll respond when I can. Got it?"

There were positive mumbles and nods, and the group trooped to the front door and checked in with security. Todd was sent upstairs for his appointment with Holly Barker, while the others were told to take a seat and wait.

Todd took an elevator to the top floor and found her office. Her secretary wasn't in yet, so he rapped on Holly's door.

"Come in!" Her voice was strong as ever.

Todd opened the door and stepped in. "Good morning."

"Good morning. Take a seat."

Todd sat and waited. She looked great in her business suit, he thought. If she hadn't been his superior, he'd have hit on her a long time ago.

"I'll give it to you without adornment," Holly said. "The project you've been working on is discontinued. As you know, it was an off-the-books effort, so no records of any kind were kept of it. If you've made notes or kept any other materials, destroy them today, without exception. Neither you nor your former team members are ever again to speak of that effort, among yourselves or to any other person. Am I clear so far?"

"Perfectly clear," Todd said, his heart sinking.

"I appreciate your written evaluations of your team members, which have already been burned, and I accept your conclusions. Therefore, each of them has had his records annotated positively and will be assigned to a new operation within thirty days, one which each will, no doubt, regard as an advancement."

"Thank you for that, Holly," Todd said. "I'm grateful to you."

"Don't be grateful too soon," Holly said. "I'm not finished."

Todd took a deep breath and let it out.

"Those above you have concluded that you are an able and resourceful officer who has had a run of bad luck. They have also concluded that your talents would be best used in other than an operational position."

He was being demoted, that was clear; all that remained was to learn if it was bad enough that they would expect him to resign.

"The deputy director has had a long conversation about you with Ed Freely, the deputy director for Technical Services."

Todd frowned and his pulse increased; this, he had not expected. Were they going to bury him in the basement of the Agency forever?

"Both Lance and Ed believe you have the technical skills and personal qualities to be a success in Tech Services. This is Ed's offer: he will assign you as a tech supervisor, meaning you will oversee tech specialists who are equipping operatives for foreign assignments. He feels that you can both learn from your specialists and teach them, given your operational background.

"You will be evaluated after a year or so in this assignment, and you will either continue in that position, if Ed feels you need further experience, or, if he feels you are ready, be promoted to assistant deputy director for Technical Services.

"Personally," Holly said, "I think you have what it takes to succeed Ed as deputy director, in time, and he is due for retirement in six years. That's it, Todd. Give me your thoughts."

Todd's thoughts were that he had been handed a great gift. He had always worried about being killed or crippled on an operation, or failing abjectly. What Holly was offering was an opportunity for long-term success in the Agency. "Again, I want to thank you for your treatment of my team," he said.

"You're welcome."

"I think your offer to me is a better than fair one, and I am very pleased to accept it."

Holly smiled and stood up. "Ed Freely is waiting for my call now," she said. "I'll tell him you're on your way downstairs." She held out a hand.

Todd shook it. "Please thank Lance, too, for his recommendation."

"I'll do that," Holly said. "Good luck down there, I know you'll do well."

Todd left her office, breathing deeply and sagging with relief. As he waited for the elevator, only one thing nagged at him: Teddy Fay was still out there, and now he would have no way to stop him.

Holly went into Lance's office and sat down.

"How'd he take it?" Lance asked.

"He seemed genuinely pleased," she replied, "not to mention relieved. He was very happy about the fate of his team, and he asked me to thank you for his new opportunity."

"I think it's a good fit for him."

"So do I."

"I suspect that young Todd is relieved to be out of harm's way," Lance said. "He has always exhibited the kind of bravado that usually covers insecurity."

"I think most operational agents have insecurities," Holly said.

"Don't confuse anxiety, which is useful for keeping one on one's toes, with insecurity, which has a large element of fear and foreboding."

"A good point," Holly conceded. "Something else has always bothered me about Todd," she said.

"And what would that be?"

"He lacks charm, and I think that is an essential quality in an agent, who is constantly trying to recruit sources."

"That's an astute observation, Holly," Lance said. "It's the sort of thing I've come to expect from you, and reaffirms my assessment of your executive skills."

"Thank you, Lance. I know you'd rather not hear his name spoken, but could I get you to speculate for a moment about what might have happened if we had not come to terms with Teddy Fay, and he had continued his existence as a thorn in our flesh?"

"You're right, Holly, hearing his name is probably going to give me a rash in an uncomfortable place, but I will answer your question. It's perfectly clear that Mr. Fay is a brilliant man, one whom I would prefer to have leading my most difficult operation than out in the wild, making trouble — in Lyndon Johnson's words, 'inside the tent, pissing out, rather than outside, pissing in.' As to what could have happened if we had not agreed to stand down: well, it could have resulted in a series of minor but vexing incidents, but more likely it would have been big and very noticeable events that would have ended in the destruction of Kate Lee's career, not to mention yours and mine, and the ruining of a fine president's reputation. Is that what you wanted to know?"

"Yes," Holly replied, "and I entirely agree." She got to her feet. "I think I can go back to work now and get some things done."

"You do that," Lance said, then turned to his computer and began to type. "Oh," he said, looking up, "what's happening with Stone and Dino's investigation?"

"I saw them last night," she said. "They have a lead, but if this one doesn't pan out, their investigation will probably end there."

"They think the FBI report is correct, then?"

"I think this new wrinkle is their last chance of proving it wrong."

"Keep me posted." Lance turned back to his computer, and Holly went back to her own office.

29

Todd Bacon was escorted to the office of Edward Freely, deputy director for Technical Services, and Freely stood up to greet him. "Good to see you again, Todd," he said. "When was the last time? When we equipped you for Panama?"

"That's right, Ed, not since then."

Ed waved him to a chair. "I take it Holly Barker gave you the overview of what you're to do here?"

"She did, and I'm grateful for the opportunity and looking forward to the work."

"Well, there's plenty of it to go around. I've got a tech supervisor, Tank Wheeler, who's retiring next month, and I had been having difficulty promoting from within, when Lance brought you to my attention. I've given you a small office next to Tank's, and I'd like you to work with him until his thirty years is up. He's involved in the equipping of three operations at the moment, and there'll never be a better time for you to plunge in. After Tank's retirement party, which should be a doozy, we'll restore his office to a semblance of repair and order, and you can move into it. I've been told that you've got thirty days off coming, but I'd be grateful if you'd spend that with Tank and take the time later."

"That's fine with me, Ed."

Ed looked up. "Here's Tank now."

Todd stood up and shook hands with the very large man whom he had met only once before, at the beginning of his Panama mission.

"It's good to see you in Tech Services, Todd," Tank said. "You're going to have a good time here, I can tell you that."

"I know I will, Tank." Then they all sat down, and Tank gave him an overview of what they were doing for the three pending operations.

A little before seven that evening, Todd left the building and walked to his car. There was a note on the windshield: *Never mind the phone calls, meet us at J.Paul's as soon as you can.*

Todd got into his rental car and drove away from the Agency. He was going to need a new car, and he was thinking

Porsche. The promotion would make it easy to handle the payments, and he could drive it for a long time.

He found the pub in Foggy Bottom, and when he walked into the place, a reproduction of an old saloon, there was a shout from a big table at the rear. They were all there, and somebody handed him a double of his favorite scotch as he sat down.

"We're alive!" his number two said. "All of us. Great assignments, though we're not supposed to tell you or anyone else what we're doing."

"Then don't," Todd said, "but I'll see you all again anyway, when you come to Tech Services for your gear." He took a huge swig of his drink.

"You got Tech Services?" number two asked. "That's cushy work — interesting, too."

"Not as interesting as what you're all going to be doing," Todd said, "but I'll never have to pull a stakeout on a cold night again, or save one of your asses from something dire."

"I'll drink to that," someone said, and they all did.

"And we'll never have to worry about what's-his-name again," Todd said, "and by the way, that name is never again to be mentioned by any of us, not even to each other. Everybody got that?"

There were grumbles and nods.

"That's the way the cookie crumbles," said number two.

"The cookie doesn't exist," Todd said. "Not anymore." He tossed off the rest of his scotch. "Now, who do I have to fuck around here to get another drink?"

"That would be me," said a pretty waitress at his elbow. That got a big round of applause.

Todd watched appreciatively as she went back toward the bar for his drink.

"Watch it, Chief," one of his men said.

"I am, pal, I am."

Teddy Fay worked away at his airplane in his hangar at Clinton Field. He borrowed a small crane from the airfield's shop and spent the morning unbolting his engine from the airframe and lowering it into a crate, for shipment back to the manufacturer. The engine had served him well, but it was near the end of its Time-Between-Overhauls period, and he had elected, for reasons of speed, to replace it with a factory remanufactured engine, which came with a zero-time logbook and a full warranty. The new engine would arrive the following day.

Teddy also had plans to replace most of the instruments in the airplane's panel with new glass cockpit instrumentation.

Teddy screwed the lid of the crate into place and affixed a shipping label. The engine would be picked up the same day. He was having the propeller overhauled locally.

Lauren called down from upstairs. "The movie starts at two," she said.

"I'll get cleaned up, and I'll buy you lunch," he called back.

He went upstairs, used grease remover on his hands and scrubbed his nails, then he took a shower and changed clothes.

Lauren was waiting in the almost new Toyota convertible he had bought her the day before, and he got into the passenger seat. "Take me for my first spin," he said.

They drove across the ramp, past the FBO (Fixed Base Operator), where they stopped to let a Cirrus pass in front of them, on the way to parking. Teddy exchanged a wave with the instructor, sitting in the righthand seat. "I've talked to that guy a couple of times," Teddy said to Lauren. "He's trying to get me to become a part-time instructor here. The FBO has a busy little flying school."

"Why don't you do that?" Lauren asked,

driving behind the airplane toward the exit gate.

"Tell you what I'd rather do," Teddy said. "I'd rather teach you to fly."

"Me, fly?"

"I think you'd enjoy it. As soon as I get the airplane back together, let me give you a few lessons. If you don't like it, we'll forget about it." Teddy was concerned about her becoming bored in their new location.

"Okay, I'll give it a whirl," she said.

They drove out to a mall, lunched at a little restaurant, and went to see *The Social Network.* They both thought it was great.

Back at Clinton Field, they let themselves through the security gate with the card they had been given, then had to slow again for the same plane they'd seen earlier.

"That student seems to be taking two lessons a day," Teddy said. "That's quite a load of work."

"He must have a lot of time on his hands," Lauren said. "Maybe he's too rich to work."

"Maybe so," Teddy replied.

30

Stone and Dino sat in a borrowed office in the West Wing of the White House and gazed at the middle-aged Filipino woman who sat across the desk from them. She was fidgeting a little, and there was a film of perspiration on her forehead. She was the fourth of the four White House maids who cleaned the family quarters, the first three having been a waste of time to question.

"Mrs. Feliciano," Stone said, "we'd like to talk with you for a few minutes about your work."

"I try very hard to do the best job I can," the woman said. "I hope there haven't been any complaints."

"Oh, no," Stone said, "nothing like that. We're just interested in some of the visitors you may have encountered in the family quarters."

"Does the president know you're talking to me?" the woman asked.

"Yes, he does. We're speaking to you at his request."

"The president told you to talk to *me?*" Now she looked more nervous than ever.

"No, Mrs. Feliciano, not just you. We're talking to all the maids who work in the family quarters to get a few questions answered."

Her shoulders slumped in relief. "Well, I don't know anything," she said. "I just clean."

Stone smiled and tried again to put her at ease. "How long have you worked at the White House?" he asked.

"Twelve and a half years," she replied.

"And how long have you cleaned the family quarters?"

"A little over three years."

"Good. Now think back over the past two years or so. Have you, when you were cleaning upstairs, ever seen anyone in the quarters who did not belong there?"

"Oh, no, sir, the Secret Service people would never allow any unauthorized persons in the quarters."

"How about authorized persons, like the cooks and repairmen?"

"Oh, yes, I see them all the time."

"How about Mr. Kendrick? Did you ever see him in the quarters?"

"Mr. Brix? Oh, yes, many times."

"What would he be doing when you saw him?"

"Well, he would sometimes bring in people from the outside, like to install new carpets or curtains, or he would supervise when they put in a new TV, or once, a new ice machine."

"Did you ever see Mr. Brix in the quarters with a lady?"

"Sometimes the people he brought in would be a lady."

"Did you ever see Mr. Brix and a lady go into or come out of one of the upstairs bedrooms?"

The woman looked more thoughtful. "Sometimes."

"Do you remember who any of the ladies were?"

"He sometimes brought the White House decorator upstairs."

"And what is the decorator's name?"

"Miss Charles," she replied. "I don't know her first name."

"Did you ever see Mr. Brix take Miss Charles into one of the bedrooms?"

"I guess . . . I'm not sure." Then her face changed, as she seemed to remember something. "Oh," she said, "do you mean go into a bedroom and close the door?"

"Did you ever see Mr. Brix and Miss Charles go into a bedroom and close the door?"

"No," she replied, "but once I . . ." She flushed a little.

"Go on, Mrs. Feliciano."

"I don't want to get anybody in trouble," she said.

"Don't worry, no one will get into trouble."

"Well, once I saw that happen, but it wasn't Miss Charles."

"Who was the lady?"

"I don't know. I went upstairs once to bring some linens that had come back from the laundry. It was early in the afternoon, when I'm not usually in the quarters. I clean in the mornings."

"Go on."

"Well, I was in the linen closet, putting away some sheets, and I heard some voices — a man and a woman. They were laughing. I stepped out of the closet just in time to see two people go into the Lincoln Bedroom. One of them, the man, was Mr. Brix."

"And the other?"

"I couldn't tell. I just saw her back for a second before Mr. Brix closed the door."

"Think back. Is there anything at all you

can remember about the woman? Tall or short? Heavy or slim? Blonde or brunette?"

She closed her eyes for a long moment, then she opened them. "No," she said.

"What did you do then?"

She looked a little embarrassed. "I won't get into trouble?"

"No, Mrs. Feliciano, you won't get into trouble. Please be honest with us, this is very important."

"Well . . . I went into the bedroom next door, into the bathroom that's just next to the Lincoln Bedroom, and I . . ."

"Go on."

"Well . . . I picked up the tooth glass and put it against the wall and put my ear to it. I could hear them talking."

"And what were they saying?"

She flushed even more. "They . . . it was sexy talk."

"Can you repeat exactly what they said? Don't be embarrassed, it's important."

"I heard her say, 'I want it,' and he said, 'Don't worry, I'm going to give it to you.' And then they were on the bed. I could hear the bed squeaking. I think they were . . . doing it."

"What do you think they were doing?"

"What a man and a woman do in the bedroom."

"Did you hear them say anything else?"

"No, just noises, like. Happy noises."

"What did you do then?"

"I cleaned the glass, then I got out of the quarters. I didn't want to be there when they came out of the bedroom."

"Did you see them after that?"

"No, sir, I didn't. But the next morning, I changed the sheets in the Lincoln Bedroom. They were . . . stained, sort of."

"Can you remember anything else, Mrs. Feliciano?"

She looked down. "I took something," she said. "From the Lincoln Bedroom bathroom."

"What did you take?"

Mrs. Feliciano's purse was in her lap, and she opened it and rummaged around for a moment, then she held out something.

Stone took it from her and examined it. It was a lipstick tube, and the name "Pagan Spring" was printed on it.

"I didn't think she would be coming back for it," Mrs. Feliciano said.

"No, I suppose not," Stone replied. "Do you mind if I keep this?"

"No, please do," she replied. "It isn't mine, anyway, but I liked the color."

"One more thing, Mrs. Feliciano," Stone said. "Can you put a date to when this happened? Estimate when it was?"

"I know exactly when it was," she said. "It was the day Mrs. Kendrick and Mr. Brix died. It was the last time I saw Mr. Brix."

"Thank you, Mrs. Feliciano," Stone said. "You've been a very big help."

The woman gratefully fled the room.

"Okay," Dino said, "your theory is starting to look a little better."

31

Stone called Holly on her personal cell phone.

"Hello?"

"Hi, it's Stone."

"Well, hello, stranger. How long has it been?"

"Uh, night before last?"

"Oh, right. I'm beginning to feel that I'm on a Stone-restricted diet."

"Well, I wouldn't want you to feel deprived. How about tonight?"

"What did you have in mind?"

"Room service and what you once so charmingly referred to as a 'bounce.' "

"Oh, yes, I think I remember."

"I should bloody well hope so," Stone said, contriving to sound hurt.

"Ah, yes, it's coming back to me, now. That sounds like a good plan. You know those vodka gimlets you make at home?"

"I believe I recall the consumption of

vodka gimlets."

"Do you think you could make some for tonight?"

"I think I can manage to remember the recipe."

"Oh, good. What is the recipe?"

"You'll have to screw that out of me tonight, so to speak."

"I'll look forward to it. Is eight o'clock all right? I have to clear my desktop of some crap."

"Eight will be just long enough for the gimlets to get frosty, before your arrival."

"Until then, then."

"Until then." Stone hung up. "Oh, shit," he said aloud to himself, then pressed the redial button.

"It's me again," she said.

"It's me again, too. I forgot to ask you about something."

"Does it involve national security?"

Stone thought about that. "I don't know, but, as Fats Waller used to say, 'One never knows, do one?' "

"Unlike yourself, I'm not old enough to remember who Fats Waller is, or was."

"Was. The composer of 'Honeysuckle Rose' and a very great pianist."

"Oh, yes. What was it you wanted to know?"

"Do you have any contacts at the DCPD?"
"That depends."
"Depends on what?"
"Whether what you want to know from them is important enough for me to use up a favor over there."
"Well, it's important to *me,* since they may very well still consider me a suspect in the murder of Milly Hart. Is that important enough to use up a favor?"
"Hmmmmm."
"Don't be coy. You don't want me arrested before tonight, do you?"
"Perhaps not. What do you want to know?"
"Do they still consider me a suspect in the murder of Milly Hart, and are there any new developments in that case?"
"That's two favors."
"Be cagey."
"I can do that, I suppose."
"You do it better than anybody I know."
"That's high praise, coming from you, slick."
"I meant being cagey."
"What a disappointment!"
"I'll do my best to make it up to you."
"Good. Suckle you later, honey." She hung up.
Dino looked across the room at him. "I

can only imagine her side of the conversation," he said.

"Dream on," Stone said, then picked up the phone again and called room service.

"Yes, Mr. Barrington?" a woman's voice said. "Or is it Mr. Bacchetti?"

"Right the first time," Stone said.

"What may room service serve you?"

"A bottle of your cheapest vodka and a bottle of Rose's sweetened lime juice."

"Is that dinner for one or two?"

"That's cocktails, honest. I'll order dinner later."

"I'm afraid our cheapest vodka isn't very cheap," she replied. "Just between us, you'd do a lot better at a liquor store."

"But then I'd have to go to a liquor store."

"May I make a recommendation?"

"Of course."

"Call the bell captain and have him send a bellman around the corner for your order. Tip him fifty dollars, and you'll save a hundred and fifty."

"What a grand idea! Why didn't I think of that?"

"Because you've obviously never bought a bottle of spirits from hotel room service before."

"You're absolutely right."

"Is there anything else we can do for you?"

"Yes, you could send up canapés for two." His attention was attracted by Dino, who was waving both hands. "Make that for three."

"Hot or cold?"

"Room temperature."

"It will be done. Good evening, Mr. Barrington."

"Good evening." They both hung up. Stone called the bell captain, and twenty minutes later a bellman appeared at the door with a brown paper bag, grinning in anticipation. Stone handed him a hundred and took the bag.

"Thank *you,*" the man said, then dematerialized.

Stone went to the bar and looked around. "We don't seem to have a measuring cup," he said.

"Do we have a shot glass?" Dino asked.

Stone looked further. "No."

"How much vodka do you have to pour out of the bottle?"

"Six ounces."

"Stop at the top of the label," Dino said.

Stone found a tumbler and poured the six ounces into it, then he refilled the bottle with the Rose's and held it up to the light. "That looks perfect," he said. "Where did you learn that?"

"From you," Dino said.

"When?"

"One night when we had finished a bottle of gimlets and you had to make some more. You had a measuring cup that time, but you were still sober enough to notice that, after pouring out six ounces, the vodka level was at the top of the label. You weren't sober enough to remember it, though."

"Now I know why I hang around with you," Stone said, tucking the bottle of gimlets into the freezer compartment of the bar fridge.

"Nah," Dino said, "you hang around with me to learn, not to remember."

Stone held up the tumbler of spare vodka. "What am I going to do with this?"

"You'll think of something," Dino said.

32

Holly took the first sip of her first gimlet. "Wow," she said. "Super cold!"

"Colder than ice," Stone said, "because alcohol freezes at a much lower temperature than water — that's the point. You don't have to water it down by putting it in a cocktail shaker with ice." He offered her a canapé.

She chose something with smoked salmon on it. "Yum."

Stone took a sip of his gimlet. "I concur in your judgment of this drink."

"Great minds, and all that."

"What did you find out from the DCPD?"

"I thought you'd get around to asking that," she said, taking another pull at her gimlet.

"What, did you think I asked you over here for the sex?"

"God, I hope so."

"Come on, cough it up."

"The detective lieutenant I spoke with expressed considerable disappointment," she said.

"In what was he disappointed?"

"He was disappointed that he couldn't find a way to hang the murder on you."

"Well, gee, the poor guy. Maybe I should send him roses, or something."

"Or something."

"What else did he say about the case?"

"In addition to being disappointed, he was relieved."

"Relieved that he couldn't hang it on me?"

"No, relieved that he couldn't hang it on Paul Brandon, Muffy's spouse. Mr. Brandon is very prominent and well connected locally, and he could have created all sorts of problems for the department if they'd charged him. They were very pleased that there was no substantive evidence against him."

"Well, I'm so happy Mr. Brandon has been spared their further attention. Do they have any fucking idea who killed Milly?"

"Oh, you and Milly were on a first-name basis, were you?" she asked archly.

"Oh, yeah, I mean we knew each other for a good twenty-four hours."

" 'Knew,' in the biblical sense?"

"Come on."

"She was, after all, a very beautiful woman," Holly pointed out.

"I can't argue that point."

"Do you think her death has anything to do with your investigation?"

"Of course I do. As a result of speaking to her, Dino and I are conducting a new round of questioning of people who work in the White House. We're talking with Brix Kendrick's former secretary tomorrow."

"And what do you expect to learn from her?"

"More about Brix Kendrick, and who he was fucking in the White House."

"I'm sorry, I must have missed something."

Stone told her about the questioning of Mrs. Feliciano.

"So she found the lipstick!"

"Yes, and Dino is giving it to Shelley so the FBI lab can do its thing."

"You think they'll find something on the lipstick a year later?"

"Once again, I refer you to Fats Waller."

"And what she saw in the family quarters happened on the same day the Kendricks died?"

"The very same day. Mrs. Feliciano was very specific about that."

Dino finished his drink and stood up. "If

you'll excuse me, Shelley and I are dining out tonight." He held up the lipstick in a plastic bag and dropped it into his coat pocket.

"Don't do anything we wouldn't do," Holly said.

"There isn't anything you wouldn't do," Dino said, then left.

"Hungry?" Stone asked, handing her a room service menu.

"Ravenous," she replied, pinching his cheek.

The following morning, Stone and Dino met with Brixton Kendrick's former secretary, Charlotte Kirby.

"I believe we spoke on the phone," Stone said.

"That's correct," she replied. She was an interesting-looking woman — in her early forties, he reckoned.

"And how long have you worked for Fair Sutherlin?"

"About seven months. After Mr. Kendrick's death, his replacement wanted to bring his own secretary with him, so I stayed just long enough to get her up to speed, then I accepted an offer to work for Ms. Sutherlin."

"Tell me, Ms. Kirby," Stone said, "were

you aware that Brix was conducting at least one affair in the White House?"

She froze. "And where did you get that idea?" she asked.

"From someone who saw him with a woman in the family quarters."

"I can't believe Mr. Kendrick would do something so outrageous."

"Were you aware that he was sleeping with women other than his wife, not necessarily in the White House?"

She glanced at her nails. "I guessed that he was," she said.

"On what evidence?"

"Mr. Kendrick took long lunch hours, something that's very rare in the White House. He would sometimes disappear in the afternoons, too. He'd say that he was 'making the rounds' of the property. He'd be gone for a couple of hours, and he wouldn't answer his cell phone."

"Ms. Kirby," Stone said, "did Brixton Kendrick ever have an affair with you?"

Her mouth fell open. "That's preposterous," she said.

"We know now that he was having affairs, and you're an attractive woman," Stone said. "What's so preposterous?"

"That anyone would think *I* would do such a thing."

"Not that Brix would."

"He was his own person, he didn't ask my permission for the things he did."

"Did you ever know or suspect the names of the women he was sleeping with?"

"Well, there were rumors about the Hart woman," she said, disdain creeping into her voice. "That's the business she's in, or so I hear."

"You heard wrong, Ms. Kirby. Milly Hart had affairs, but not for money."

The woman shrugged. "If you say so."

"Any other names? Particularly in the White House?"

"The White House staff is, in some ways, like any other group of workers. These things happen."

"With whom did they happen, in the case of Mr. Kendrick?"

"I wouldn't know," she said, in a manner that made Stone think she knew. "Is that all?"

"For the present, Ms. Kirby. Thank you for your help."

Her reaction, as she stood to leave, made Stone think she was happy she hadn't helped too much.

33

The following morning, early, Stone and Holly were having breakfast with Dino and Shelley, when the phone rang. Dino got up and answered it. "For you," he said to Shelley, holding up the phone. "It's the FBI lab."

Shelley left the table and went to the phone. "Yes?" She listened. "You got both? That's great. Have you run them against the database? Thank you very much!" She hung up and returned to the breakfast table.

"Come on, tell us," Stone said.

"This is your lucky day," Shelley said. "The lab got both a fingerprint and a DNA sample."

"Any idea whose?"

"They ran it against the database and got a hit on a White House employee."

"Who?" Dino asked, hanging on her every word.

"One Esmerelda Feliciano."

"Shit," Dino said.

"Why aren't you happy?" Shelley asked.

"Because Feliciano is the White House maid who found the lipstick. I guess she's been using it ever since."

"We should have expected this," Stone said. "I refuse to be disappointed."

"You go right ahead and refuse to be disappointed," Dino said. "I'm pissed off."

They ate for a couple of minutes in silence. Finally, Holly spoke. "I'm going to have to try that lipstick. The people who wear it do such exciting things. What's it called?"

"Pagan Spring," Dino said.

Holly began laughing, and soon they were all laughing.

"Where do they get these names?" Shelley said.

"Marketing and advertising people sit around having what they like to call 'brainstorms' and make them up."

"Are they drunk when they're doing this?" Shelley asked.

"I wouldn't be surprised."

The phone rang again, and again Dino got it. He pointed at Stone. "It's for you, this time."

Stone got up and went to the phone. "This is Stone Barrington."

"It's Fair Sutherlin."

"Good morning. This is a pleasant surprise."

"First of all, thank you for your thank-you note. I was glad you could come to my dinner party."

"I was glad, too. We all had a good time."

"Are you free for dinner this evening?"

"Ah, yes."

"Come for a drink at my house at seven, and we'll go on from there. Dress casually."

"Thanks, I'll do that."

"Oh, I almost forgot my original reason for calling: Paul Brandon's wife, Muffy, was murdered early this morning."

Stone didn't speak for a moment.

"Hello?"

"I'm here. Where did this happen?"

"At her home. You were there earlier, I believe."

"Yes, I was. Where was Paul Brandon at the time?"

"Attending a conference on government and business in Chicago, at the request of the president."

"I see. How did you hear?"

"A Lieutenant Padgett from the DCPD called me at home five minutes ago. He said the murder bore striking similarities to that of Milly Hart."

"When did it happen?"

"Between five and six this morning."

"Thank you for letting me know," Stone said.

"See you at seven."

"Yes." Stone hung up and went back to the table.

"You look kind of funny," Dino said.

"Well, I don't feel very funny," Stone said. "That was Fair Sutherlin, from the White House. The D.C. cops called her a few minutes ago and told her that Muffy Brandon was murdered early this morning."

"Where was Paul Brandon?" Dino asked.

"In Chicago, sent by the president to attend a meeting."

"Too bad," Dino said. "If he hadn't had an alibi, we might have cleared two murders in one fell swoop."

"Fair said the cops said the two murders resembled each other."

"Well," Dino said, "if you're a murderer, and you've got a technique that's working, why change it?"

Holly burst out laughing. "You sound like you're talking about somebody's golf swing."

"Golf swing, ball-peen hammer swing, what's the difference? It's all muscle memory."

"Actually, it was a claw hammer," Holly said. "At least that was the tool in the Hart murder. Lieutenant Padgett told me."

"Time for you to do me that favor again," Stone said.

"Call the D.C. cops?"

"Right. It was Padgett who called Fair, so I guess he's on the investigation."

Holly looked at her watch. "It's pretty early," she said.

"Padgett is already at work, remember?"

"Oh, yeah." She got up, went to the phone, made the call, and came back. "It's almost exactly like the Milly Hart murder," she said, "even to the appearance of the wounds."

"Who found her?" Stone asked.

"A housekeeper, who was sleeping downstairs. She came up to start breakfast and found Mrs. Brandon in the entrance hall, in her nightgown."

Dino nodded. "Killer rings the bell, Muffy gets out of bed and answers the door, killer whacks Muffy and leaves."

Stone looked thoughtful. "Seems to me I remember from our visit to the house that there was an intercom for the doorbell, and they had a multiline business phone system, same as mine in New York."

"So?" Holly asked.

Dino spoke up. "So, Muffy Brandon knew her killer. Why else would she get out of bed and go to the front door? If it had been the milkman or the newspaper boy, she'd have told him to fuck off and then gone right back to sleep."

"Good point," Holly said.

"I wonder how many other women Brix Kendrick was sleeping with?" Stone said.

"Why do you care?" Holly asked.

"Because it's a group of women who are dying at an alarming rate," Stone said. "I'd really like to know if there were others, so they can be warned."

"How are you going to find out if there were others?" Holly said. "Brix is dead, and so are the only two other women you know he was sleeping with. So is his wife, who might have known."

"I don't think we're going to find out who the others might be," Dino said.

"Why not?" Holly asked.

"Because if there were others and someone knew about them, we'd have heard about it at Fair Sutherlin's dinner party the other night. The people there seemed to know *everything*."

"It's Washington," Stone said.

34

Todd Bacon went over his checklist again, reading it aloud so Tank Wheeler could see that he had forgotten nothing. He walked down the long table, pointing at items and checking them off his list.

"Perfect, Todd," Tank said. "You're in the groove already. Now let's get those two officers down here and go over it all with them." Tank picked up a phone and spoke to someone. "They're on their way," he said.

"Tank," Todd said, "did you ever work with Teddy Fay when he was here?"

"Sure I did. Teddy trained me. He must have put me through hundreds of quizzes like the one you've just gone through. Teddy was terrific at briefing agents, and a genius at anticipating what kind of equipment they would need. He invented a big chunk of the electronic stuff that we still use to equip field people."

"I heard that he was important to the

department," Todd said.

"He was more than important, he was essential. The Agency tried everything to get him to stay on, but he retired right on time. He'd made a bundle inventing kitchen and household gadgets that got sold on television in the middle of the night, so he could afford a happy retirement."

"I heard that, too," Todd said.

"Funny, they're still selling some of his inventions, and I guess they got someone to replace him who could come up with the gadget ideas, because you turn on the TV when you can't sleep, and they're selling them right now."

That notion stuck in Todd's mind, but he had to push it to the back of his brain, because the two young officers arrived for their briefing. The man looked to be in his mid-twenties, though Todd knew he was probably older, and the girl appeared to be no older than eighteen or nineteen, though she was probably older, too. Todd thought it was brilliant casting for the mission.

Todd and Tank introduced themselves, and Todd began the briefing. "Here are your passports," he said, handing them each one. "You've already committed your legend to memory, and the dates in the passports are the ones you've memorized. You're university students at Leeds, in the English Midlands, and you're hiking in the mountains east of Beirut." He picked up a small leather case and handed it to them. "This is a perfectly ordinary GPS navigator, made by Garmin, their latest model. When you activate it in Beirut, it will already have your track from England in memory, where a good tech can extract it. That will help support your legend, if you're interrogated."

Todd held up two smaller, flatter boxes. "These are the GPS units that really matter. When turned on, they will broadcast an encrypted position that will tell us exactly where you are, even if you're separated. You'll hide this on your body: you, Jim, will glue it behind your scrotum; you, Carey, will put it inside your vagina. Those are the places least likely to be searched, but don't count on their not being found. If you are arrested, hide them in the room where you're being held and turn them on. If rescue is an option, these units will help make it possible."

He continued the briefing, holding up each piece of equipment, demonstrating it when necessary, then passing on to the next item. "Nothing you're carrying will identify you as anything but what you say you are, from your passports to the contents of your wallets."

When he had finished the briefing, he held up two foil-wrapped condoms. "These are your way out, if everything goes wrong. Inside is a flat vinyl-encased container holding a small amount of a clear liquid. You can conceal it in your mouth, between the cheek and the gum. It won't dissolve, but if you bite it hard, the liquid will spill, and you'll have only seconds to live. As you were told in your training, it will always be your decision as to whether or not to use it, but if things get so bad that you no longer want to live, it's there."

Todd watched as the two packed their clothes and equipment into their backpacks, then he shook their hands and sent them on their way.

"That was good," Tank said. "You didn't sugarcoat it."

"How can you sugarcoat taking your own life?" Todd asked.

"Joke about it. That was what I did in the beginning, but Teddy Fay brought me up short and told me to be direct with them. I felt better about it when I was."

That brought Todd's mind back to where it had been before the briefing. In his pursuit of Teddy, the man had never seemed short of money. He had bought and discarded cars along the way, and that took cash. Teddy must still be designing those kitchen gadgets, he figured, and he still had a way to get them on TV and get paid for them. Exploring that might lead to finding him.

Then Todd stopped himself. *I can't go on obsessing about Teddy Fay,* he told himself. *That part of my career and my life is over, and it's not a good idea to revisit it.*

He joined Tank in the cafeteria for lunch, and put Teddy Fay out of his mind.

35

Stone arrived at Fair Sutherlin's apartment and was greeted with a kiss to the corner of his mouth, with just a little tongue. Fair was dressed in tight jeans and a V-necked cashmere sweater that showed an inviting amount of cleavage, and her breasts seemed unfettered under the sweater.

"I had a tougher day than I had planned," she said, "so do you mind if we just order in some Chinese?"

"Fine with me," Stone replied.

She handed him a menu. "You choose, and order too much so I'll have leftovers to keep me alive for a few days. I'll get the trays ready." She disappeared into the kitchen.

Stone consulted the menu and noted that Fair had checked the dishes she preferred, probably on an earlier occasion. He chose the marked dishes that he liked, too, and called the restaurant, ordering pork pot stickers, shrimp balls, Yang Chow fried rice,

General Tso's chicken, orange beef, sweet-and-sour shrimp, and Mongolian beef, then he went to the bar. Fair had been drinking scotch on his previous visit, so he poured her a Chivas Regal and found some Knob Creek for himself, then he took the drinks into the kitchen.

Fair was arranging trays containing napkins, silverware, wineglasses, and little individual salt and pepper shakers. He handed her the scotch. "That looks beautiful," he said of the trays. "When I order Chinese at home, I tend to eat straight out of the cartons."

"I do that, too," she said, "when there are no witnesses." She took a gulp of her scotch. "Thanks for remembering," she said.

"Thanks for having my bourbon." He took a sip. "How did you find your way to the White House?" he asked.

"When I was a senior in college, at UVA, I volunteered to work for a Democratic candidate for Congress, as research for an eventual thesis for a master's degree in political science. To my surprise, I thoroughly enjoyed the experience, and the congressman-elect offered me a job on his staff. I didn't take it, but I had met some interesting figures in the party during the campaign, one of them Tim Coleman, the deputy chief of staff for Senator Hart, who gave me his card and told me to keep in touch. Just before I graduated, Tim called and invited me to come to Washington for a talk. He introduced me to the senator, whom I admired, and they talked me into forgetting my master's and joining the Hart staff.

"I began as deputy press secretary, and after a couple of years of that Tim got promoted to chief of staff, and I became his deputy."

"That sounds like a wonderful opportunity," Stone said.

"I got lucky," she replied. "When Senator Hart died, Tim went to the White House, and the senator's appointed replacement hired me to be his chief of staff. The guy knew nothing, and that made me look like I knew everything, but I have to say, I did a good job for him. That led to a job in the press office at the White House, during Will Lee's first term, and when he got reelected, Tim Coleman moved me over as one of his two deputies."

"So you've been in the White House for how long?"

"Nearly seven years."

"It must seem like home by now."

She laughed. "It seems like a sweatshop."

"Will you be glad when it's over, and Will Lee goes home to Georgia?"

"I suppose I'll have mixed feelings," she said.

"Any plans for after the White House?"

"I've got my eye on a House seat in Virginia," she said. "I don't think the guy is going to run again, and I think I'd be good at it."

"And after that, what? Governor? Senator? President?"

She gave him a sly smile. "Who knows where the road may lead?"

The house phone buzzed, and she told the doorman to send up the food. Stone met the deliveryman at the door, paid him, and brought the big bag into the kitchen. Fair gave Stone a bottle of Chardonnay from the fridge to open, then they heaped food onto their plates and took their trays into the living room.

Fair switched on the TV. "Do you mind? I TiVo the evening news."

"Not at all."

They watched the news silently, and Fair spoke only when fast-forwarding through the commercials. When it was over, Stone said, "I thought there might be a mention of the Muffy Brandon murder."

Fair shook her head. "Nope, that's a local

story. If Paul Brandon were still in the Cabinet, it might have made the national cut."

"Since you worked for Senator Hart, you must have known his wife."

"Milly? Sure. She was in and out of the office all the time. I liked her."

"How about Muffy Brandon?"

"I met her a few times at dinner parties. I liked her less. She was too skittish for my taste, too brittle. She was beautiful, of course, but, as far as I was concerned, not an attractive person."

"Any thoughts about who killed them?"

She looked at him in mock surprise. "Are you kidding? You're the investigator: you tell me."

Stone watched her closely for her reaction to his next statement. "I think the killer may very well work in the White House."

She choked on her wine. "Are you *serious?*"

"I am."

"Please, *please* tell me why you think that."

"Things have come out in our latest round of interviews with White House people."

"What things?"

"I haven't reported to the president yet, so I can't tell you."

"Have you mentioned this to anyone outside the White House?"

"Just the people involved in our investigation."

"Please promise me you won't breathe a word of that to anyone else. It's the sort of thing that the media would go nuts over, and we'd be overwhelmed for days, maybe weeks, dealing with it. It would just make it harder for us to get our work done in the months Will Lee has left in office."

"I won't tell anyone else. It's just a theory, at this point."

"Well, it's a very scary theory," she said. "When do you plan to wrap up your investigation?"

"We were about ready to do that, until the two women were murdered," Stone said. "Now we'll have to wait and see how everything plays out."

"I wish to God Will and Kate hadn't asked you to look into Mimi's and Brix's deaths," she said. "Everything that's happened seems to be because you're here, doing this."

"Sometimes I feel the same way," Stone said.

"Enough shoptalk," she said. "I have an early day every day, so we should get into bed now." She took his face in her hands and kissed him, then she took his hand and put it inside her sweater, on her breast. "Are you game?" she asked. "I don't have time for foreplay."

"I'm game," Stone said, stripping off her sweater, while she worked on his buttons. He was astonished at how swiftly she had inflamed him.

36

Stone was wakened by an electronic beeping. Momentarily disoriented, he first thought he was at home in bed, then that he was back at the Hay-Adams. Then Fair rolled over on him and brought him fully awake.

She came quickly, then made it her business to see that he did, then she was out of bed and heading for the bathroom. "Go back to sleep," she said. "I've got an early national security briefing, but there's no need to roust you out of bed."

Stone looked at the bedside clock: just after five A.M. He felt oddly rested, then it occurred to him that they had been in bed by eight-thirty the evening before. He had had a full eight hours of sleep. He heard the shower turn on.

He got out of bed, found his clothes, and got dressed. He was combing his hair, using her dressing table mirror, when he saw the lipstick. He picked it up: Pagan Spring. He opened the cap, and it seemed almost unused. So what? he thought. It seemed to be a very popular lipstick.

He went to the bathroom door, and she was getting out of the shower. "Dry my back?" she said.

Stone grabbed a towel and rubbed her down all over, enjoying the process.

"I want to do it again," she said, "but I'm on the clock. Start the coffee, and put some muffins in the toaster oven, will you? I'll drop you at your hotel on the way to work."

Stone did as he was told, and by the time the coffee was ready, she was in the kitchen, standing while eating a muffin and drinking coffee. "You're an extremely good lover," she said.

Stone looked at her, surprised. "Thanks. So are you."

"I haven't had enough sex since my last relationship," she said. "It's the job. There's no time to meet anyone."

"I'm glad to have been of service," Stone replied.

She tossed off her coffee. "Let's go," she said. She led him out of the apartment, and they took the elevator down to the garage, where her Prius was parked.

"I would have thought they'd send a car

for you," Stone said.

"When I'm chief of staff," she replied, driving out of the garage. "The president doesn't like it when staff start ordering up White House transportation without some real need. It's easy for me to drive myself."

She stopped just short of the portico at the Hay-Adams. "You'd better get out here. We don't want to be seen together at this hour of the morning." She gave him a kiss, waited until the door was closed, then drove away.

The muffin hadn't been enough for Stone, so he ordered a full breakfast from room service. He was already eating his eggs when Shelley came out of Dino's room, followed shortly by Dino. They sat down. "When did you get in?" Dino asked.

"Late, but I woke up early and couldn't get back to sleep, so I ordered breakfast."

"And what did the evening reveal that will aid our investigation?" Dino asked.

Stone thought about that. "As far as I'm concerned, it eliminates Fair as a suspect," he said.

"Why is that?" Shelley asked.

"She's too normal to have murdered three people."

"Too normal?" Dino said. "I see murders

committed all the time by people who seem normal."

"You'll have to trust me on this, Dino," Stone said. "I can't prove she didn't do it. She worked in Senator Hart's office and knew Milly, said she liked her. She knew Muffy Brandon, too, but didn't like her. There's not the slightest evidence that she could have killed either of them. She does use Pagan Spring, though. It was on her dressing table in her bedroom."

"I checked with the drugstore chain that sells it in D.C.," Shelley said. "They've sold about nineteen hundred tubes of Pagan Spring since it came out a little over two years ago."

"Swell," Dino said.

"Since the two women were killed, my office is taking a new interest in the Kendrick deaths."

"Great," Stone said. "As far as I'm concerned, you folks can take over the investigation today, and I'll go home and practice a little law."

"Yeah?" Dino said. "I'm starting to get interested again."

"Who, specifically, is getting interested over at the Hoover Building?" Stone asked.

"My boss, Kerry Smith."

"Does he think you screwed up the original investigation?"

"Let's just say that if something comes up that contradicts our conclusions, he wants to be ready with some answers to the inevitable questions."

Dino spoke up. "I think we need to take a deeper look at Charlotte Kirby."

"Why?" Shelley asked.

"Because when we talked to her, she was very uptight, very defensive."

"That's true," Stone said. "She seemed to recoil."

"And we don't have anybody else who's recoiling," Dino said. "So she's my suspect, until she isn't."

"Agreed," Stone said.

"I'll pull her FBI file," Shelley said. "Everybody who works in the White House has one. There might be something there that will help."

"Good idea," Stone said. "Especially since we don't have another one."

A copy of Charlotte Kirby's FBI file was delivered just before lunchtime, and Dino read it first.

"Anything interesting?" Stone asked.

"She's divorced, one grown daughter."

"Gee, that's damning, isn't it?"

"She was valedictorian of her class at Vassar."

"We're lucky she hasn't murdered more people."

"And she was a suspect in a murder case four years ago, when her sister was killed. She was cleared when the sister's boyfriend confessed. He's in a hospital for the criminally insane."

Stone thought. "So she wasn't cleared by evidence, but by the confession of a lunatic?"

"That's about the size of it."

"How did her sister die?"

"Head trauma from a blunt instrument."

"I see."

"And Charlotte inherited her sister's share of her father's estate, which amounted to a couple of million bucks."

"She gets more and more interesting, doesn't she?"

"I was interested before, remember?"

"This time, let's not make an appointment. Let's just show up."

37

They arrived at the White House, and Stone told the receptionist that they were there to see Fair Sutherlin. Two minutes later, as he had hoped, Charlotte Kirby appeared.

"I'm sorry," she said, "but Ms. Sutherlin wasn't expecting you. She just left for a meeting at the State Department."

"Then we'll settle for speaking with you, Ms. Kirby," Stone said. "Since Fair's office is not in use, we can talk in there."

"I'm not sure —"

"Ms. Kirby, you should know by now that we have the run of the White House."

Her shoulders sagged. "Oh, all right. Follow me."

Stone and Dino fell in behind her, and as they walked down the hall, Stone said quietly to Dino, "Do you think she's Brix Kendrick's type?"

"I don't think Brix had a type," Dino replied. "Or if he did, it included most of the female gender."

Kirby ushered them into Fair's office and closed the door behind them. "Now," she said, "what can I do for you?"

"You can have a seat," Stone said, indicating the sofa. He and Dino took chairs opposite.

"What is this about?"

"The same thing it was about the last time we talked," Stone said, "except we did most of the talking, and you were reluctant to answer."

"I don't know anything you want to know," she said.

"On the contrary," Stone replied, "you know just about everything we want to know, but don't want to tell us."

"You knew about each and every one of Brix Kendrick's affairs, didn't you?" Dino said.

She looked alarmed, but said nothing.

"Ms. Kirby," Dino said, "if you continue to obstruct our investigation, the president is going to hear about it, then Ms. Sutherlin is going to hear about it, and then you're going to find yourself working in a government basement somewhere, if you're still employed at all."

Tears rolled down her cheeks.

Dino handed her a box of tissues from

Fair's desk. "Let's start at the beginning," he said. "When did you first meet Brix Kendrick?"

"Two years ago," she said. "At a White House staff party. I was working for the director of the General Services Administration, and Mr. Kendrick needed someone with my experience in government."

"And when did you come to work for him?"

"A few weeks after meeting him."

"And when did the two of you first have sex?"

The tears came again. "The night we met," she said.

"Where?"

"In his office, on the sofa."

"Brix was a fast worker."

"Mr. Kendrick was a very persuasive man."

"And when did you next have sex?"

"The following evening, at my apartment." Dino started to ask another question, but she held up a hand. "After that, it was three or four times a week, sometimes in the evenings, sometimes he'd come by my apartment early in the morning — five or six — on the way to work."

Stone spoke up. "And when did Brix stop having sex with you?"

She drew a deep breath and let it out slowly. "As soon as I came to work for him. He said that since we were working together, we couldn't take the chance. After that, he was all business, except when he was talking about his affairs."

"He talked with you about other women?" Dino asked.

"I know it sounds perverse, and maybe it was, but he'd talk about what they'd done in bed, and in great detail. He knew it made me . . ."

"Jealous?" Dino asked.

"Horny," she replied. "He would insist that I . . ."

"Go on."

"That I masturbate while he talked about the other women."

Dino seemed to have run out of steam, so Stone stepped in. "And how did that make you feel?" he asked.

"Less horny."

"Did you enjoy these experiences?"

"I'm ashamed to say I did," she replied. "I began to look forward to them."

"No need to feel ashamed, Ms. Kirby," Stone said. "You're telling the truth now."

"And I feel better for it," she said.

"How long did these . . . conversations continue?"

"Until the day he died," she replied.

"Now," Stone said, "let's start from the day you went to work for Mr. Kendrick: who were the women he slept with?"

"There were nineteen of them," Kirby replied.

Now Stone ran out of steam, and Dino stepped in. "Their names, please." He opened his notebook.

"He never used their names. He either made up names, like 'Shotzie,' or 'Toots,' or he gave them nicknames, like 'the Bunny,' or 'the Grasshopper.' "

"What did he call Milly Hart?" Stone asked, recovering.

"I think she was the one he called 'the Rabbit,' " she said, "but I can't be sure. He saw the Rabbit for a long time, and often."

"And what name did he give Muffy Brandon?"

" 'The Doggie,' " she said, "because that was her preferred position."

"And when, in the chain of events, was he seeing her?"

"Only for the last month or so of his life, I think. She lived in Georgetown, and he would run over there, screw her, and be back in half an hour. He said he would walk into her house, and she'd be waiting for him, already naked. He'd just drop his pants and stick it in. Ten minutes later, he was on his way back to the office."

"You make it sound as though Brix was not a considerate lover," Stone said.

"Oh, I don't mean to make it sound that way," Kirby said. "He took pride in giving them what they wanted, the way they wanted it. He was very . . . proficient. If he was seeing Milly Hart, he'd be gone for a couple of hours. She liked *everything.*"

"Ms. Kirby," Dino said, "would you describe Brix Kendrick as a sex addict?"

She laughed at that. "What else? He practically turned me into an addict, too, except I was addicted only to him."

"Did you like him?" Stone asked.

"I loved him, and I loved working for him, too. He was a good boss, and he got a tremendous amount of work done every week, in spite of his extracurricular activities. I made a lot of that possible, of course, but he always gave me a list of things to accomplish before he went out."

"Ms. Kirby," Stone said, "this is important. Early in the afternoon of the day he died, he had sex with a woman in the family quarters — in the Lincoln Bedroom, in fact. Who was she?"

"Yes, he came back, went to work, and then, a little after five, he changed and went to play tennis on the White House court."

"Who was she?" Stone asked again.

"I don't know," she said, "but he called her 'the March Hare.' "

38

Stone and Dino were quiet on the drive back to the Hay-Adams. When they were back in the suite Stone called Holly.

"Hello?"

"We've just left the White House, where we conducted a very important interview. I don't want to talk about it on the phone, so can you come over for a drink or dinner?"

"I can come over for a drink *and* dinner," she replied. "Seven o'clock?"

"Good. See you then."

Dino picked up the phone. "I think it will save time if I ask Shelley over, too."

"We may as well have all the principals here," Stone said.

Dino looked at Stone closely. "You seem a little down, pal. I would have thought you'd feel great about our interview."

"You're right, Dino, I should feel that way, but I'm sort of depressed about the direction this is taking."

"What, too many suspects?"

"Right, and nobody knows who they are, except Brix, and he took the shortcut out of here."

"Well, we know three of them," Dino said, "but two of them are dead. All we've got is Charlotte Kirby and the March Hare. That's from *Alice in Wonderland,* isn't it?"

Stone nodded. "The Tea Party. It's where the expression 'mad as a March hare' comes from."

"Well, Brix seemed to give a meaning to each of his nicknames: the Rabbit, the Doggie, et cetera. So maybe the March Hare is a nut job."

Stone nodded. "She'd almost have to be," he said. "I mean, jealousy is one thing, but to kill Brix's wife, then two of his lovers, well . . ."

"Maybe," Dino said, looking thoughtful, "the March Hare is Charlotte Kirby herself. Maybe Brix drove her crazy with all of his descriptions of his sex life. Maybe masturbation really does drive you around the bend."

"That's a perfectly valid theory," Stone admitted, "but it goes against the grain."

"What grain is that?" Dino asked.

"The grain of Charlotte Kirby. I bought her story — hook, line, and sinker."

Dino nodded. "I know what you mean. I

had the feeling that we had stripped all her pretense away and we were getting the unadulterated truth. That happens in a successful interrogation, you know? The perp finally has no place to go but the truth."

"You're right," Stone said.

"Maybe she still knows something she hasn't told us, though," Dino said. "Maybe she's holding back the final tidbit."

"The name of the March Hare?"

"Yeah."

Stone shook his head. "No, I think she would have told us, if she knew."

"Maybe she suspects?"

"I think she would have told us her suspicion. I think she's sick of all this, and she wants an end to it."

"I can't disagree with you," Dino said. "And I still think the March Hare is a nut job."

"Agreed," Stone said.

Shelley and Holly arrived, and drinks were poured. "Why so glum, fellows?" Holly asked.

"Because," Stone said, "we've had a breakthrough."

The room became very still.

"How so?" Holly asked carefully, looking from Stone to Dino.

"It's like this," Dino said. "We broke through, then found ourselves staring at another stone wall."

"Explain, please," Holly said.

Stone recounted their interview with Charlotte Kirby.

"Nineteen!" Holly exclaimed. "And if Charlotte's timeline is accurate, that's over a two-year period."

"That's about right," Dino said.

"Brix was a busy boy."

"To paraphrase Frank Sinatra," Dino said, "I don't know why he isn't in a jar at the Harvard Medical School."

"Oh, come on, folks," Shelley said, speaking for the first time, "that's less than one a month."

"Yeah," Holly said, "but he was doing it multiple times with each one."

"It's hard to know how he had the energy for tennis," Dino said, and everybody laughed. "And for all we know, he might have been doing that for years."

They ordered dinner and took a break from the case for a while. Finally, when they were on coffee and brandy, Stone spoke up. "I don't know where to go from here," he said.

"Neither do I," Dino replied.

The phone rang and Stone went to the

desk to answer it. "Hello?"

"Mr. Barrington?"

"Yes."

"It's Charlotte Kirby."

"Yes?"

"I thought of something else."

"Yes?"

"Brix had another nickname for the March Hare. He used it only once."

"Yes?"

"He called her 'RoboCop.' I'm afraid that's all I have for you."

"Thank you very much," Stone said. He hung up and returned to the table.

"Who was that?" Dino asked.

"It was Joan," he said.

"Your secretary Joan?" Holly asked.

"Right. Another brandy anyone?" Nobody wanted another. They repaired to their respective bedrooms.

39

Todd Bacon was at a Technical Services meeting at the Agency, where a schematic of a new cell phone was being displayed on a large screen as the designers presented it.

"Our phone," the designer said, "operates perfectly as an Apple iPhone Five, except that it will also broadcast a message that has been composed on the phone's keyboard, then automatically compress, encrypt, and transmit on a high radio frequency of our choosing. And, as you can see, the phone is indistinguishable from the Apple phone."

Todd's phone began to vibrate on his belt, but he ignored it. "That's obvious," he said, "but what about if you open the phone and expose the works? Is it indistinguishable then?"

"It is," the man replied, "except that the battery is marginally smaller. We've added three new chips to the phone, but each looks exactly like the ones they replaced, even to the serial numbers."

"And if you crack the parts?"

"All you'd see is circuits which, visually, are identical. What's different is what the circuits are used for, and the software contained therein."

Todd's phone vibrated again. "So if an enemy tech is really good, is he going to be able to tell the difference between your phone and the original?"

"If he's really, really good, he'll notice some differences, but he'll just think that Apple has made some changes, and if he cracks one of the three parts, the software will automatically be dumped."

"So," Todd said, "he'll find an Apple phone with no software?"

"That's better than leaving our software available for him to play with, isn't it?"

"Yes, of course it is," Todd said. "That will protect your software, but it's not going to protect my operative. They'll know immediately that he's got a very sophisticated communications device that does not work like an Apple phone."

"Well," the man said, sounding exasperated, "what do you suggest?"

"What do *I* suggest?" Todd asked. "I'm not the designer here."

The man gazed at the blowup of his design. "I suppose we could load the Apple software and our software on the same chip, and have only ours dumped."

"Is there room on the chip for all that software?" Todd asked.

"Almost," the man said. "We'll have to write some new compression code."

"Well, then," Todd said, "that's my suggestion. How long will it take you?"

"A few weeks," the man said, looking doubtful.

"And what about the battery capacity? Is it going to be sufficient for transmitting in HF?"

"If it's fully charged, and the message is brief, but if it's plugged into an electrical outlet, your transmitting would be unlimited."

"And what about the antenna?"

"It's contained with the original antenna, but you'd have to send from outdoors or near a window."

"Then find a way to supplement that antenna so that we can send from indoors. Sounds like you've got a lot of work to do, gentlemen," Todd said. "Find a way to do it in a few days." He stood up. "Thank you very much. We'll see you here, same time next week, and we'll expect a bug-free working model. And if you're going to make the battery smaller than the original, you'd better print something on it that indicates that it's a Mark Two."

Everybody got up and shuffled out of the room. Todd's phone was still vibrating.

Once out of the room, Todd checked the phone; his old number two was calling. He pressed the number to return.

"Yeah? Todd?"

"Don't call me on this phone," Todd said.

"But I've got something important to tell you."

"All the more reason not to call me on this phone." He broke the connection and returned to his office.

It was nearly seven o'clock when Todd finished his summary of what he had seen at the tech presentation, and he was very tired. All he could think of was a large scotch, a TV dinner, and bed. He left his office and took the elevator to the garage, where he had a favored parking spot. He drove out to the gate, checked out there, and headed toward the apartment he had rented.

As he hit the main road he saw a car's headlights appear in his rearview mirror. It was some distance back, but he reacted the way he'd been trained to. He accelerated, and the headlights disappeared, then the cell phone on his belt vibrated.

Todd looked at the calling number. "Yes?" he said into the phone.

"There's a rest stop ahead. Pull into it."

It was number two again. Todd pulled into the rest stop and got out of the car, his hand on the pistol under his jacket.

A black SUV pulled in behind him and switched off its lights, then the door opened. "Relax," a voice said, "you know who I am." He got out of the car and approached, his hand out.

Todd ignored the hand. "You're breaking protocol," he said. "The rule is no contact."

"You wouldn't talk on the phone," the man said. "This is the only way I could reach you, and it's important."

"What's so important?" Todd asked. "And this better be good."

"It's about Teddy Fay," the man said.

Todd turned and started back toward his car without a word, but the man caught his arm and spun him around.

"Am I going to have to fight you to stop this nonsense?" Todd asked. "You know that's a dead issue."

"Listen to me, then do what you like," number two said.

Todd's shoulders sagged. "All right, what is it?"

"I've got my private pilot's license now," he said, "and I've been training for my instrument training over at Clinton Field. It's just the sort of airport Teddy likes."

"What's your point?" Todd asked angrily.

"Twice I've seen a couple in a black Toyota convertible at the airport. I asked around, and they're living in a hangar there. A guy named Karl Walters bought it six or seven years ago, but he hasn't been around much. Now he's living there with a girl."

"And you think it's Teddy? You wouldn't know him if he stepped on your foot."

"You're right about that, Todd."

Todd made to leave, but the man stopped him again.

"I don't want to hear this," Todd said.

"I don't care whether you want to hear it or not, I'm going to say it. You're right, I wouldn't know Teddy from Adam, and both times I've seen the car, the reflection on the windshield kept me from seeing the driver."

"You haven't even seen him, but you think it's Teddy? Jesus, I was obsessed with the guy, but you're even worse."

"I know the girl," number two said. "I followed her in San Diego. It's Lauren Cade. And where she is, Teddy is."

Todd sighed. "I'm going to let this go," he said, "but if I hear from you again about this or anything else, I'm going to bust you with Lance Cabot. Do you understand me?"

The man shrugged and walked back to his car without another word. In a moment, he drove away in a spray of gravel.

Todd got back into his car and sat, his forehead pressed to the steering wheel, his heart pounding. Finally, he started the car and resumed his trip home. "I'm forgetting this," he said aloud to himself. "I'm putting it right out of my mind."

40

Stone and Holly were sitting up in bed having breakfast the following morning when Stone's cell phone buzzed on the bedside table.

"Dad? It's Peter."

"Peter! How are you?" Peter and Ben, Dino's son, were in their first year at the Yale School of Drama. "I haven't heard from you in a couple of weeks."

"I know, I've got a play opening soon, and it's been crazy here."

"I expect so."

"I was hoping you'd be able to come up for the opening?"

"I'd really love to do that, Peter, but I'm in Washington, D.C., working on something really important, and I don't think I can get away."

"So this is that murder at the White House, and those other women?"

Stone was stunned. "How on earth can

you know that?"

"Haven't you seen the morning papers? We get the *Times* delivered, and it's on page eight."

Stone covered the phone and turned toward Holly. "Will you please get the papers from the front door?" She got out of bed and padded, naked, into the living room. "How long is the play going to run? Maybe I can get up later."

"Only four nights, through the weekend. Tell me about this thing you're working on, Dad. It sounds like there might be a film in it."

"Oh, no, no, no," Stone said. Holly returned with the papers. "The *Times,* page eight," he said to her, and she began looking.

"Why not? It's public property now."

Holly shoved the paper in front of him. "Hang on, I've got the paper here." Stone read the article, which took up half a page. "It appears," he said to Peter, "that the *New York Times* knows as much about this case as I do."

"The *Washington Post,*" Peter said. "That's where the *Times* got the story."

"Oh, yeah, I see that now."

"When the play closes, Ben and I want to

come down there and hear about this first-hand."

"You stay right where you are, young fellow. You've got school to do, and Dino and I are up to our ears in all this." Holly took the paper from him and started to read.

"Oh, all right, but when I'm back in New York or when you're up here, I want to know everything."

"All right, when it's all over I'll give you the details."

"I've got to run, Dad, it's dress rehearsal today."

"Take care of yourself, Peter." Stone hung up.

Holly put down the paper. "I don't believe this. They've got Charlotte Kirby's story, and your interview was only yesterday."

"I don't believe it either," Stone said. "Charlotte would never have told a newspaper reporter all that. The White House must be going nuts." The cell phone rang again, and Stone picked it up. "Hello?"

"It's Fair Sutherlin," she said. "The White House has gone nuts over this story. What were you thinking, talking to the papers?"

"I haven't talked to the papers, and neither has Dino. Do you think we're insane?"

"Charlotte had to be sent home from work, and I don't know how she can go on working here with this hanging over her head. How could you?"

"I'm telling you, I didn't!" Stone said, with some heat.

"Who knew about this besides you and Dino?"

"Just the principals in the investigation, nobody else. I haven't even had a chance to tell the Lees."

"Think, Stone: how could this have gotten out in all this detail?"

"I suppose Charlotte could have talked to somebody."

"It wouldn't be in her interests to do that," Fair pointed out.

"I know, you're right. Look, I've only just seen the papers. Let me get back to you when I know more." He hung up before she could speak again.

Stone got out of bed, walked across the living room, and hammered on Dino's door. "Dino! Get out here, we've got trouble!"

"All right, all right," came the muffled reply.

Holly had gotten into a robe and followed Stone with the paper, then Dino came out of his bedroom in pajamas, looking sleepy. "What?" he said.

Holly handed him the paper. Dino sank into a sofa and began to read. "What the fuck?" he said, finally.

"Where's Shelley?" Stone asked.

"She slept at home last night. She left right after you and Holly disappeared."

"She's the only other person besides the three of us who knew about our conversation with Charlotte Kirby."

"Oh, come on, Stone, you know better than that. Shelley would be jeopardizing her career by blabbing to the press about this."

"You'd think so," Stone said, "but we know it wasn't any of the three of us. Who else knew about Charlotte Kirby?"

"Charlotte Kirby did, dummy," Dino said. "She must have talked to somebody."

"Isn't there stuff in the story Charlotte didn't know?" Holly asked.

Dino shook his head. "We were at a dinner party the other night where everybody at the table seemed to know most of it. But Charlotte would have been the only person who knew about her story."

"Let's go see Charlotte Kirby," Stone said. "Where's the FBI file? Her address is in there."

"On the coffee table," Dino said, reaching for the phone. "I want some breakfast first, and I need a shave and a shower."

"So do I," Stone said.

Holly went into the bedroom, then called

out, "Your cell is ringing again."

Stone went back into the bedroom and answered it.

"This is the White House operator," a woman's voice said. "Will you speak to the first lady?"

"Of course," Stone said.

"Stone?" Kate Lee said.

"Mrs. Lee, I know why you're calling."

"I should think you do. What on earth is going on?"

Stone looked at Holly; he needed to hand off this call.

"I'm not here," Holly whispered.

"We haven't found out yet, but we're working on it. May I call you back later today, when I should know more?"

"Oh, all right," she said, "but it had better be good." The first lady hung up.

"Oh, shit," Stone said. He sat down on the bed and put his face in his hands.

41

Dino drove, while Stone worked the car's navigator and Holly sat in the rear seat. The sexy woman's voice directed them, turn by turn, to a pleasant street in Arlington, Virginia.

"Uh-oh," Holly said, "look up ahead."

There were two large vans parked on the street in front of a nice split-level house, and there were half a dozen other cars, as well. The lawn was populated with men and women with cameras, microphones, and notebooks. "Oh, Jesus," Stone said.

"Pull over here," Holly said, when they were three or four houses away.

"Aren't we going in?" Stone asked.

"Are you kidding? After that story in the papers this morning, every reporter here has a photo of you and Dino in his pocket. You'd be manufacturing a whole new headline."

"I see your point," Stone said.

"Further to my point," Holly said, "they don't have a photo of *me* in their pockets, and I'm not going to give them the opportunity to take one."

"So, what do we do?" Dino asked.

"Just sit tight for a minute," Holly said, taking out her cell phone and dialing a number. When it was answered, she identified herself. "I need a street cleaned, and right now," she said. She gave the address of Charlotte Kirby's house. "Two TV vans, half a dozen cars, and a dozen reporters and technicians. Soonest. And I want the street blocked for the rest of the day, except for identified residents." She hung up. "It'll be a few minutes," she said.

"You can do that?" Dino asked. "Block a street and throw out the media?"

"Let's just say *someone* can do it," Holly replied. "You and I don't need to know whom."

"Who," Stone said drily.

"Oh, shut up."

Stone leafed through his copy of the *Times,* folded the Arts section back to the crossword, uncapped his pen, and started in.

"He does that every day," Dino said.

"Don't I know it?" Holly replied.

"In ink," Dino said, "just to annoy me."

"I wish you two had brought your own crosswords," Stone said. "Now, be quiet so I can think."

"You need quiet to think?" Holly asked. "You wouldn't make it as a CIA officer."

"And you never finish a crossword," Stone said.

They sat quietly in the car for another ten minutes, then two Arlington police cars drove into the street from opposite ends, their lights flashing, no sirens. The cars stopped, and four officers emerged and engaged the crowd on the lawn in conversations. Voices were raised, arms were waved, and insults were shouted, but the crowd eventually was swallowed up by their respective vans and cars and drove out of the block, whereupon the two police cars took up station at each end of the street.

"I think we can go in now," Holly said.

"That was very neatly done," Dino said admiringly as he drove to the house and pulled into the driveway. "If I tried to do that in New York, I'd end up in stocks."

"We can do it in New York, too," Holly said, getting out of the car.

The three of them walked to the front door of the house and Stone rang the bell. Nothing happened. Stone stepped back and regarded the house. A lamp was on in a window, but there was no other sign of life.

"She's not going to answer," Dino said.

Holly started to walk to the rear of the house. "Wait here," she said.

Stone and Dino leaned against the wrought-iron railing of the porch and waited. "She's going to break in," Dino said, "isn't she?"

"They teach them that at the Agency," Stone replied.

The front door opened and Holly waved them inside. "Mrs. Kirby invites you in," she said. "She's in her bedroom, if you'd like to follow me." Holly led them to a bedroom door, opened it, but stopped them before they could enter. "Let's preserve the scene for the local cop shop."

Charlotte Kirby was sitting up in bed, but her head had rolled to one side. The wall behind the bed and a picture hanging on it were spattered with blood and brain matter, and there was a hole in the picture.

"From what I can see," Dino said, "self-administered gunshot wound to the head, via the mouth. Fairly small caliber."

"I concur," Stone said.

"So do I," Holly replied.

"Why is it that everybody we need information from in this case either offs himself or somebody does it for him?" Stone asked plaintively.

"I've noticed that," Holly said drily, taking out her cell phone and pressing a speed-dial number. "Okay," she said, "time to get the locals in here. They'll need a wagon and a crime-scene team. Looks like a suicide." She hung up.

"I don't see a weapon," Stone said. "Can't I just tiptoe in there and look around for it?"

"Absolutely not," Holly replied. "They've been nice enough to clear the street for us, so we're not going to fuck up their crime scene by way of thanks."

"Oh, all right," Stone said.

"If somebody fired the shot for her, they'll still find a gun," Dino said. "The March Hare is not stupid, that much we know."

"Oh," Holly said, "I think poor Charlotte had plenty of reason not to want to ever leave her bed again."

"I'll bet there's a diary in the bedside drawer," Stone said.

"I'd certainly like to find out," Dino replied. "Holly?"

"Don't point that thing at me," Holly said. "You want to tiptoe in there and take a peek, it's on your head."

"Nah," Dino said, "it's on Stone's head. He's the only one here who doesn't have a government job to hang on to."

"Oh, all right," Stone said. He slipped off his shoes and tiptoed across the rose-colored carpet to the bedside table and, with his pen, engaged the drawer pull and slid it open. He poked around in the drawer with the pen, then closed it and tiptoed back to the door. "No diary," he said. "Just condoms, lubricant, and tissues."

"Charlotte was ready for anything, wasn't she?" Holly asked.

Stone started down the hall, back toward the front of the house.

"Where are you going?" Holly asked.

"I want to see what else is in this house," Stone replied.

Dino followed, producing a pair of latex gloves from a pocket and donning them.

Holly trailed the two. The three of them stood in the neat living room and looked around, then Stone walked into what turned out to be a den.

There was a desk and some bookcases and a filing cabinet. "You do this one, Dino," Stone said. "You're gloved."

Dino started with the filing cabinet. "Bills, tax returns, a file of clippings from travel magazines," Dino said, after a minute's look.

"Try the desk," Stone said.

Dino walked to the desk and opened the three top drawers. "Bingo," he said.

42

Someone hammered on the front door. Holly went to answer it, and Dino stuffed the diary under his belt in the small of his back. Holly returned with two police detectives and a couple of people with satchels. Holly directed them to the bedroom, but one detective remained with them.

"So," he said to Holly, "I know who you are. Who are these two?"

"Lieutenant Dino Bacchetti, NYPD, and Stone Barrington, NYPD, retired."

The detective nodded. "I read the papers. This got something to do with that lady from the White House?"

"The corpse in the bedroom is the lady from the White House," Holly replied.

"Be right back," the detective said. "You three stay here." He walked down the hall toward the bedroom.

"Don't you dare give him that diary," Holly said to Dino.

"I hadn't planned to," Dino replied.

The detective returned. "How come you're gloved?" he asked Dino.

"Because I'm the only one carrying gloves."

"What did you touch with those gloves?"

"I had a look in the filing cabinet in the study and in the top desk drawers."

"What did you find?"

"Nothing I'd want in my scrapbook."

"Did the lady have a diary?"

"I looked in the bedside drawer," Stone said, "and there was no diary. I didn't touch anything, though. Your people have a clean shot at prints."

"Gee, thanks," the detective said. "Suppose I print all of you, anyway?"

"Suppose you go fuck yourself," Dino said.

"Now, gentlemen," Holly interjected. "Everybody be nice. Detective, I'll confirm that nobody touched anything."

"How'd you get in the house?" he asked. "The front door was locked."

"The back door isn't," Holly said, careful about her use of tense.

"You spooks don't run the Arlington PD," he said.

"We have neither the time nor the inclination," Holly replied. "We're grateful for your help."

Stone spoke up. "You should be grateful," he said to the detective.

"Oh? Why's that?"

"Because if she hadn't made the request, you'd have two TV trucks out there and a yard full of reporters clamoring for a statement."

The detective made a mock curtsy in Holly's direction. "Thanks for keeping my picture out of the papers. The chief might have seen it."

"Here's an idea," Dino said. "Why don't you call them back in?"

"Good idea," the detective replied.

"Detective," Holly said, "I don't think you need us anymore."

"Christ knows that's true," he replied. "Good afternoon and good riddance."

Holly herded Stone and Dino out the door. "Let's move," she said. Then, when they were outside: "Dino, don't let that diary fall down your pants."

They were back in the suite at the Hay-Adams before Dino produced the diary. Holly grabbed it, sat on the sofa, opened it to the last page, and read aloud.

" 'Those two from New York grilled me

relentlessly this afternoon. I told them everything, and it was embarrassing, but it turned me on. Took care of that when I got home. Now I'm depressed.' "

"She doesn't sound all *that* depressed," Dino said, "not if she could do herself after our conversation."

"I never knew being interrogated was a turn-on," Stone said.

"I'm taking that as a compliment," Dino replied.

Holly was turning pages, scanning them. "My goodness, she described every sexual encounter with Brix, even the masturbatory ones!"

"Was she sleeping with anybody else besides Brix?" Stone asked.

"Apparently not," Holly replied.

"Then the paraphernalia in her bedside drawer was just in case?"

Holly closed the diary and tossed it to Stone. "This only goes back to the first of last year. She must have earlier ones."

"I don't think it's worth trying to get them out of the Arlington cops," Stone said. "Not if this one covers the time leading up to the deaths of Brix and his wife."

"You can read the whole thing," Holly said, rising. "I'm going back to the office."

"Why don't you brief the director," Stone

said. “I’m not ready to face her again.”

“What can I tell her?”

“Tell her we’ve hit a brick wall. Tell her all our possible witnesses are dead.”

“I’ll do that,” Holly said, then took her leave.

“There’s one still alive,” Dino said when she had gone. “The March Hare.”

“Well,” Stone said, “if you’d like to introduce me to her, I’ll be glad to ask her all the right questions.”

“I think you already know her,” Dino said.

“Yeah?”

“Sure, she’s somebody at the White House, and you know who you know there.”

“Fair Sutherlin?”

“Who else?”

“I don’t buy it.”

“Who else you got?”

Stone shrugged. “We can’t nail her for all this just because we don’t have another suspect.”

“Stone, do you remember ever having been a cop?” Dino asked.

“Vaguely.”

“What does a cop do when he’s eliminated all the suspects but one, but he doesn’t have any evidence?”

“You want us to interrogate Fair?”

“Why not? I’d beat her with a telephone

book if I could get away with it."

"I don't think my heart would be in it," Stone said.

"I think you're referring to another part of your anatomy," Dino said.

"You think that just because I slept with her, I'd give her a pass?"

"I can't think of any other reason for you to give her a pass," Dino said. "Tell me one."

"I just don't think she's capable of all this. Under the political hard shell, she's a decent person."

"That's not an assumption I'm willing to make," Dino said. "Call her."

43

Fair Sutherlin's new secretary showed them into her office. "Hey, fellas," she said, waving them to the sofa. "What's up?"

"You already have a new secretary?" Dino asked.

"They're lined up, wanting to get into the West Wing," Fair replied. "It only took a phone call. I hear you went out to Charlotte Kirby's house, just in time to discover the body."

"Yes," Stone said, "we always seem to get places just a little late."

"What did you find?"

Dino snorted. "You mean you haven't seen the crime-scene photos yet?"

"Actually, I did. They were e-mailed to me. I've never seen anything quite like that. I've only got twenty minutes, fellas, and you've already used up five. What do you need?"

"Just some answers," Dino said.

Stone crossed his legs and looked at a picture on the wall across the room. "Is that one from the National Gallery?" he asked.

Fair started to answer, but Dino cut her off.

"Never mind that. You were in the White House when Brix's wife's body was found, weren't you?"

"Don't you remember our last conversation about that?" she asked irritably.

"Indulge me."

"I'm at the White House every day of my life," she said, "weekends included, and a lot of nights, too. Ask me if I killed her."

"Did you kill her?" Dino asked, following instructions. "Even accidentally?"

"No. What else?"

"But you knew her."

"Asked and answered the first time we talked. Listen, do you think that by asking me the same questions over and over, you're going to get different answers?"

"I've known it to happen," Dino said.

"Well, this is not a police interrogation room, and I'm not the perp, so don't try that shit with me."

"Shall I tell the president you said that?" Dino asked.

"Tell him anything you like," Fair said, shrugging. "Now, let's cut to the chase, fellas. We're busy around here saving the country."

"Saving it from what?" Stone asked.

"Whatcha got?" she asked. "We'll save the country from it. We do that every day. Some days, we save the world."

"How did that story about us interviewing Charlotte Kirby get into the papers?" Dino asked. "And don't tell me it's Washington."

"It's Washington," Fair replied.

"Did you give it to somebody?"

"I did not. Did it ever occur to you that Charlotte might have given it to somebody?"

"And then offed herself because it was in the papers?"

"Stranger things have happened in this town. What's going on here?"

Stone spoke up again. "We've run out of people to interview. You're the last witness standing."

"Witness? Witness to what?"

"You tell us," Dino said.

Fair looked at her wristwatch. "You've got one more question. Make it a good one."

Stone looked at Dino. "Yeah, make it a good one. I'm on tenterhooks."

"All right," Dino said. "Who do you think killed the Kendricks?"

Fair sighed. "I think Brix killed them

both," she said, then stood up. "Now get out of here. I'm not talking to either of you anymore." She looked at Stone. "Unless there's a drink and dinner involved."

Stone and Dino shuffled out of her office, and the door slammed behind them.

"That was pretty lame," Stone said.

"Yeah, and you were such a great help," Dino replied.

"It was your party. I didn't want to talk to her in the first place."

"You mentioned that."

They walked down the hall and out to the car.

"You still think she's the March Hare?" Stone asked.

"Who else is there?" Dino asked.

"There must be seven or eight hundred people working in there," he said, jerking his thumb toward the West Wing. "We didn't talk to all of them."

"Are you proposing that we talk to just the women?" Dino asked.

"Suppose the March Hare is a man? Suppose Brix swung both ways?"

"Of all the people we've talked to," Dino said, starting the car, "did any one of them say a single word to indicate that Brix had the slightest interest in fucking anything but every female who got in his way?"

"Now that you mention it, no. Are we going back to the Hay-Adams?" Stone asked as they drove out the White House gate.

"That's where my stuff is," Dino said. "The stuff I've got to pack before I can go home."

"You're giving up?"

"Give me one really good reason to continue, and I'll stay."

Stone was quiet.

"Well?"

"We know the March Hare exists."

"We know that Charlotte Kirby told us the March Hare exists," Dino said. "That's it."

"You think she was lying?"

"Everything we know about her so far indicates to me that she was crazy enough to make it up."

Stone shrugged. "Certainly her behavior was, to say the least, eccentric."

"Eccentric? That's all you got?" Dino asked. "The woman was a self-operating nymphomaniac. She was a thick slice of fruitcake, chock-full o' nuts."

"All right," Stone said, "I'll give you all of that. But if you're right, here's my theory."

"I gotta hear this," Dino said.

"Charlotte killed Brix's wife, and she was the woman the maid heard with Brix in the

Lincoln Bedroom. She killed Milly Hart and Muffy Brandon, too."

"And herself," Dino said. "Don't forget herself."

"Her motive was jealousy of Brix, and she took herself out of the picture just as he did, and for the same reasons."

Dino turned into the portico of the Hay-Adams. "I like it," he said, switching off the engine. "Now, let's go upstairs and write a report that says just that, then get the hell out of town before somebody else gets offed, making fools of us both."

"Done," Stone replied.

As they walked through the door, the phone was ringing. Stone got it. "Hello?"

"It's Holly. Dinner with the Lees in the family quarters at eight. Shelley Bach and I are commanded, too."

"What do they want?"

You know what they want, and you'd better have it ready."

"See you there," Stone said. He hung up and turned to Dino. "We're dining with the Lees. Let's get that report together."

44

Stone and Dino met Holly and Shelley at White House reception, and they rode up in the elevator together, all of them quiet.

Will and Kate Lee were sitting in the family quarters' living room when the Secret Service agent ushered the group in. Hands were shaken, drinks were ordered from the butler.

The president spoke first: "From what I hear, you fellows are about done with your work."

"We are, Mr. President," Stone replied. He handed the president a brown hotel envelope. "Here's our report," he said.

The president dropped the envelope on the coffee table before him and took a sip of his drink. "I'd rather hear it from you."

Stone looked at Dino. "Go," Dino said.

"Mr. President, Mrs. Lee," Stone said. "We have been unable to prove conclusively, with the available evidence, who is responsible for all that has occurred. All we can offer you is an opinion that is supported by what we have learned, and it would never stand up in a court of law."

The president took another sip of his drink. "Kate and I are prepared to accept your conclusions and get on with our work and our lives. Let's have it."

"We believe that the key to what has happened is Brixton Kendrick's former secretary, Charlotte Kirby," Stone said. "We believe that she killed Emily Kendrick with an edging stone from the White House garden. She and Mr. Kendrick had been having an affair for some time, and her motive was jealousy. After that, the available evidence supports suicide by Mr. Kendrick."

"Charlotte Kirby!" Lee said, half to himself. "I hardly knew her, but she seemed such a mild person."

"She was anything but, Mr. President, from her own testimony, which we've outlined in our report."

"And the other women?"

"All killed by Charlotte Kirby," Stone said, "who then took her own life."

Kate Lee spoke up. "So there's no one left to prosecute or blame?"

"That's correct," Stone said. "We believe

Ms. Kirby was more than a little mad, and as you will see in our report, she was probably made that way by Brixton Kendrick."

"I just have one question, Stone," the president said. "If I had not initiated your investigation, would Milly Hart and Muffy Brandon still be alive?"

"There's no way we can know that, Mr. President," Stone replied. "It's very possible that Charlotte Kirby would have gone on her killing spree even if we hadn't turned up. You are in no way to blame for her actions. That's in our report, too."

"Perhaps I'll feel better about this after I've had time to digest it," Lee said.

The butler came into the room. "Mr. President, Mrs. Lee, dinner is served."

They went into the dining room and Kate Lee directed them to their seats. Her husband tasted the wine, and dinner began.

"Stone," Kate Lee said, "I suppose you and Dino will be returning to New York soon."

"Tomorrow morning," Stone said.

"I expect you'll be glad to get home," the president said.

"I'll tell you truthfully, Mr. President, the practice of law has never looked more attractive than it does now."

"As does New York City police work,"

Dino added, "as opposed to the D.C. brand."

"I can understand that," Lee said.

"Our visit here has been an education," Stone said.

"Kate and I are grateful that you took the time to come down here. We thought your investigation would ease our minds, but I'm afraid it's just given us more to grieve over."

"I'm sorry for that, Mr. President."

"Don't be. We've learned to take things as they come. One of the first things that struck me after I took office was how little I could affect what happens. Presidential power is often an illusion. Kate, on the other hand, sees the effect of her work more immediately than I do. She runs an operation — it succeeds or fails. In order to get that kind of closure, I have to veto a bill."

The sound of a ringing telephone came from the living room.

"I don't like it when that phone rings in the evenings," Lee said. "It's never good news."

The butler came into the dining room. "Assistant Director Bach," he said, "your office is calling. They say it's urgent."

Shelley rose. "Excuse me, Mr. President, Mrs. Lee," she said, then left the room.

"Stone," the president said, "what is your

work in New York like these days?"

"Well, my two largest clients for a while were Strategic Services, the security company, and my wife's affairs."

"We were very sorry to hear of her death," the president said.

"Thank you, sir. I also spend a good deal of time supervising the legal work for an insurance group, Steele, that came to us recently."

"I understand you get called upon by Lance Cabot from time to time," Kate said.

"I'm afraid so," Stone said wryly. "Sometimes I'm sorry I signed that contract with your agency."

Kate laughed. "I suppose you've learned that our work isn't great fun."

"Perhaps not," Stone said, "but it's always interesting."

"Dino," the president said, "what keeps you occupied these days?"

"Well, Mr. President, even though New York City crime is down in almost every area, we still have enough murders, rapes, and robberies to keep my detectives in the Nineteenth Precinct busy."

Shelley Bach returned to the dining room. "Mr. President, Mrs. Lee," she said, "I've just had word that Fair Sutherlin has been murdered."

There was a loud clink as the president dropped his fork onto his plate. "Where? How?" he asked.

"She was bludgeoned to death in her apartment, apparently late this afternoon," Shelley replied. "Her body was discovered by her building superintendent less than half an hour ago, and, knowing that she was a federal employee, he called the FBI. My people are on their way to the scene, and, if you'll excuse me, I have to go over there now."

"Of course," the president said. He and his wife stood and shook her hand. "Stone, Dino? I expect you'll want to go there, too."

"Yes, sir," Stone said, standing. He and Dino said their good-byes.

"Holly," Kate Lee said, "you'd better go, too. I want a full report as soon as possible."

The four left the quarters and got into the elevator.

"I don't think we're going to be able to pin this one on Charlotte Kirby," Stone said as they rode down.

45

They arrived at Fair Sutherlin's apartment building and took the elevator upstairs. The door to her apartment stood open, and men in suits were inside.

"Wait here a moment," Shelley said. She took latex gloves, a hairnet, and booties from her handbag and donned them, then disappeared inside. A moment later, an agent appeared and issued the same equipment to Stone, Dino, and Holly.

"Careful, aren't they?" Dino said. "Most cops would just blunder into the place."

Fair Sutherlin's body lay under a sheet in the living room.

Shelley called a man over. "This is Special Agent Dave King," she said, "the supervisor on this investigation."

"I thought that was you," Holly said.

Shelley shook her head. "Dave and his people are homicide specialists. I'm just a bureaucrat, as far as they're concerned."

"That's not true," Dave King said to them. "Assistant Director Bach always sees something we don't. We're happy to have her at a scene."

Shelley made a motion with her hand, and Dave King stooped and pulled back the bloodstained sheet. Fair's face bore an expression of surprise. The eyes were open, the right side of her head was crushed, and her hair was matted with blood.

Stone turned away, feeling horribly sad.

"Maybe this homicide isn't connected to the others," Holly said.

"That's nice of you, Holly," Stone replied, "but it's clear that Dino and I backed away from this too soon."

"Thanks, Holly," Dino said, "but Stone's right."

Shelley spoke up. "If this is connected, and I'm inclined to think it is, then Fair must have been having an affair with Brix Kendrick, too. All the other victims were."

"We never turned up any evidence to connect her to Brix," Stone said.

"Just one more thing we missed," Dino added.

Dave King brought over a large clear plastic bag containing what appeared to be a marble statuette, covered with blood. "The murder weapon," he said.

"That's a weapon of opportunity," Dino said. "Indicates her murderer didn't necessarily come here to kill her. Indicates anger, too. But it wasn't a burglary gone wrong. I'll bet nothing's missing."

Fair's large handbag, tagged, sat on the floor near her body.

"Anything missing from that?" he asked Dave King. "Money? Credit cards?"

"The bag seems to be intact," King replied.

"May we look in the bedroom?" Stone asked.

"Sure, just don't move anything."

Stone walked into the bedroom and looked around. It seemed the same as it had been on his earlier visit. Her tube of Pagan Spring lipstick was still on the dresser. So much for clues, he thought.

Dino walked to the dressing table and raised the lid on a jewelry box. "Some nice pearls," he said, "and a few rings and bracelets."

"You're right," Stone said, "it wasn't a burglary."

There was a scream from the other room, and they both ran back there. The young woman who had shown them into Fair Sutherlin's office earlier stood in the doorway, being consoled by Shelley Bach, who finally got her quieted down.

"Who are you?" Shelley asked.

"My name is Rose Marie Dyvig," she said, and spelled the last name, as if she were accustomed to doing so. "I'm Ms. Sutherlin's secretary. One of them."

"Dino and I can confirm that," Stone said.

"I came to check on her," the young woman said. "She got a call on her cell phone late this afternoon and left the White House, saying she'd be back in an hour. I waited for her, because I had some papers to deliver that needed her signature. Finally, I called her a couple of times, and when I didn't get a reply and when she didn't come back, I came over here."

Shelley sat her down and turned to Dave King. "Did you find her cell phone?" she asked.

"No, there wasn't one anywhere in the room — not in her handbag, either."

"The murderer took it," Dino said, "so we couldn't check it to see who called her this afternoon."

"That was very thorough," Stone said. "I wonder what else she took."

"Why do you think it was a woman?" Holly asked.

"It's the March Hare," Stone replied.

"Who else?" Dino asked.

"I don't think there's anything more we can do here," Shelley said. "Let's get out and let my people do their work."

Shelley walked Rose Marie Dyvig to her car, parked at the curb, then Stone and Dino went to the Agency SUV that they had been loaned, and Shelley and Holly to their respective cars.

"You ladies may as well join us for dinner at the Hay-Adams," Stone called out. They both nodded and got into their cars.

"Have you told the hotel we're checking out tomorrow?" Dino asked.

"No."

"Just as well. Looks like we're not going anywhere."

Room service did its usual fine work, and they dined without much chat. After dinner, the two couples adjourned to the bedrooms and closed the doors.

Stone and Holly lay naked in bed, holding hands, but they had not otherwise touched each other.

"You seemed familiar with Fair Sutherlin's apartment," she said. "Did you sleep with her?"

"Yes," Stone said. "Once. Dino and I went to a dinner party there, too."

"Don't get the idea that I mind," Holly said.

"Thanks for not minding."

"We don't have that kind of relationship," Holly said. "What was your impression of her?"

"I liked her. I admired the way she did her work."

"Do you think she had an affair with Brix Kendrick?"

"On no evidence but the manner of her death, yes."

"I wish I had met the guy," Holly said. "I'd like to see what sort of man could string together that many affairs and get away with it in a town where everybody talks about everybody."

"You could argue that he didn't get away with it," Stone said. "He's dead, after all."

"Do you think the March Hare killed Charlotte Kirby?"

"We never saw a gun, did we? I certainly want to see the police report. Can you get it for me?"

"Better if Shelley does that," Holly said. "She has an official reason to ask for it, and I don't."

Stone chuckled. "That doesn't seem to stop you from getting what you want from the cops."

"Better not to ask too often," Holly said. She raised herself onto one elbow. "Stone, do you have any idea, any thoughts at all, about who the March Hare is?"

"No," Stone said. "Not an idea, not a thought."

"That's depressing."

"Tell me about it."

46

Stone and Holly emerged from the bedroom to find Dino breakfasting alone. "Shelley had an early meeting," he said. "Your breakfast is on the sideboard."

Stone and Holly helped themselves from the hot dishes and sat down. "I wanted to ask her to get us the police report on Charlotte Kirby's murder," Stone said.

"I already thought of that. She'll fax it over to us."

"Good man," Holly said, looking at him funny. "You seem depressed, Dino. Not your usual cheerful self."

"Dino, cheerful?" Stone said, laughing.

"I thought we were out of here this morning," Dino said. "We're not."

"That is depressing, isn't it?" said Stone.

"I don't mind having you two around," Holly said. "You put a little fun into my humdrum life."

"Humdrum my ass," Dino snorted. "The

stuff you get into at the Agency, you're probably having too much fun!"

"I wish we had some sort of lead — anything," Stone said. "I don't know what to do next."

"How about Fair Sutherlin's cell phone?" Dino suggested. "It's disappeared, and the murderer must have taken it."

Holly spoke up. "The Agency has a program for cell phone searches," she said. "Can I use your laptop, Stone?"

"Sure, it's on the desk."

Holly sat down at the computer and began typing. "I'm logging on to the Agency mainframe," she said, "then I can access the program." She stopped. "There. What's her number?"

Stone got his iPhone, looked up the number, and read it out.

Holly typed in the number, then waited, looking at the computer screen. "It's searching."

"You could use that program at the NYPD, Dino," Stone said.

"We've had it for years, or something like it. Comes in useful now and then."

Holly checked the screen again. "Nothing."

"Maybe it's been removed from D.C.," Stone suggested.

"No, this would find it anywhere in the world, unless it's been smashed, the SIM card removed, or it's where there's no cell reception, like in a bomb shelter."

"So much for Fair's cell phone," Stone said.

The fax machine on the desk rang and began spouting paper.

"It's the Arlington PD's report on Charlotte Kirby's killing." He picked up the small stack of papers.

"Charlotte was a federal employee. Why isn't Shelley's bunch handling that?" Dino asked.

"Maybe that's only in D.C., not Virginia," Holly said.

"So, Stone, what does it say?"

"Single gunshot wound to the head, probably self-inflicted. A Walther PPK/S .380 found at the scene."

"I didn't see a gun, did you?" Dino asked.

"No, and I went to the bedside and opened the table drawer, so I was close enough."

"Maybe it fell off the bed or got tangled in the covers," Holly offered.

"No evidence of the presence of another person in the room," Stone said. "Looks like a straight-up suicide to me."

"I'll buy that," Dino echoed.

Stone handed Holly the file, and she began to read through it. "Here's something: they found a box of ammo in her underwear drawer, with six missing. The gun had five in the magazine, and there was a single empty cartridge on the bed."

"There you go," Dino said. "She did herself."

"Do you think Charlotte knew more about the March Hare than she told us?" Stone asked.

"She poured out everything else," Dino said. "Why would she hold back on that? She must have hated whoever it is."

"Holly," Stone said, "does it say anything about prints on the ammo box?"

Holly flipped through the reports. "Here it is: no prints on the box or on the ammo in the magazine or on the magazine. Charlotte's prints were on the gun."

"Now that's interesting," Stone said. "How did Charlotte load the gun and leave no prints on the magazine or cartridges?"

"Either she wore gloves, or she wiped them," Holly said.

"Why would she do either of those things? After all, she was about to kill herself. Why would she care about her prints?"

"The March Hare would care," Dino said, "pardon my rhyme."

"All the others suffered blunt trauma," Holly said. "Why is Charlotte different?"

"My guess is, the March Hare lay in wait for the others," Dino said, "but she found Charlotte in bed and it was easier to shoot her."

"Did they run the gun, Holly?" Stone asked.

Holly consulted the file. "Bought used, at a gunshop in Richmond, Virginia, the year before last. Buyer named G. B. Smith, whose address was a phony."

"Virginia is notorious for phony gun sales," Dino said. "We see the results on the streets of New York all the time."

"We're knocking ourselves out for nothing," Stone said. "The March Hare is careful, we already know that."

"Tell you the truth, I thought Fair was our woman," Dino said. "I didn't like her attitude yesterday."

"I never thought so."

"Yeah, I know," Dino said, "she was too nice."

"No, just too straightforward. She had a full life — she didn't have time to go around murdering people."

"So," Dino said, "we've got a very careful serial killer."

“Looks that way,” Stone said. “And that’s all we’ve got.”

47

Teddy Fay and Lauren Cade lay naked on the beach at Gay Head, on Martha's Vineyard. It was Sunday afternoon. Most of the other nudists, all locals, with beach parking permits, had gone. Teddy and Lauren had sneaked down the trail from the parking lot and had managed to blend in with the couples and families who had been enjoying the sun on their bodies. They had enjoyed a long weekend in a B and B in Edgartown.

They packed their dirty dishes into the picnic hamper, folded their blanket, then got back into their clothes. It was a bit of a hike up the cliffs, and they were puffing a bit when they got to the car.

Teddy got the rental started and they began driving to the airport.

"You know," Lauren said, "this island might make a better place to live than D.C. It's lovely here."

"It is," Teddy agreed, "but remember, it

has a New England winter, and what with one airport and a ferry to deal with, it's a hard place to get out of, should we have to leave in a hurry."

"You're right," she said. "But let's find a place that has a good climate year-round, and where escaping our pursuers isn't such a problem."

"We had a place like that in La Jolla," Teddy said. "The San Diego weather was great year-round, but we were run out of there."

"But you did say they aren't pursuing us anymore," Lauren pointed out.

"That's what they agreed to," Teddy said. "Now we have to find out whether they really meant it, and to do that without getting caught we have to be ready to move on a moment's notice."

"For how long?"

"A year, maybe."

"Or we could just go now," Lauren said.

"If we went now, where would you want to go?"

"How about Asheville, North Carolina?" she asked. "I was there once, and they seem to have a good year-round climate, not too hot in the summers or too cold in the winters."

"That's not a bad idea," Teddy said.

"Maybe we could fly down there next weekend, if the weather cooperates, and take a look at it."

"That would make me feel as if we're doing something," Lauren said, "not just waiting for something terrible to happen."

"Nothing terrible is going to happen," Teddy said. "Not if we go on being careful."

"I just can't get over the feeling that we're living too close to the Agency, that sooner or later we're going to bump into someone from your past that we'd rather not see."

"I know, baby," Teddy said, patting her on the knee. He pulled into the little Vineyard airport. They parked the car in a rental slot and left the contract and the keys with the rental car agency. They stowed their luggage in the airplane, and Teddy did his usual careful preflight inspection of the airplane.

They took off to the south, headed back to Clinton Field, in D.C., and their comfortable hideout hangar. Teddy figured to be on the ground there before dark.

Todd Bacon landed at Clinton Field in the Agency's Bonanza, usually kept at Manassas Airport, in Virginia, and taxied to the FBO, where he ordered fuel. There were two airplanes ahead of him, waiting for the fuel truck. The delay would give him time to have a look around.

Late on a Sunday afternoon, students were still doing touch-and-goes, and pilots based at the field were coming back from weekends away. Todd strolled nonchalantly over to the rows of hangars, where airplanes were being put away.

His number two had been fuzzy on which hangar he suspected of being Teddy's, so as he walked, he mentally eliminated the ones where he could see the owners taking care of their airplanes.

Todd wore a baseball cap and sunglasses; he didn't want to be noticed among the locals, especially by Teddy himself. He had not been able to keep the couple out of his thoughts, and he knew that coming here was against the clear instructions that Holly Barker had given him to think of Teddy as dead. He wasn't even sure what he would do if he came face-to-face with the old man. He was armed, sure, but Teddy would be, too, and he couldn't get into a gunfight in a place like this.

As he came to the end of a row of hangars he looked up and saw, silhouetted against the setting sun, a Cessna 182 RG on final for the runway. Same airplane as Teddy's, but of course it was a different color. This one was two tones of blue, with red stripes, not a factory-issue paint scheme.

He watched it touch down, then brake and turn off the runway, and in the moment of that turn, the setting sun illuminated the pilot. He wasn't young, and, like Todd, he was wearing a baseball cap and dark glasses. Todd couldn't say he recognized him, since he had never seen Teddy up close, but there was a younger woman seated next to him, and he had seen her before, he thought, in San Diego.

Todd stood at the corner of the row of hangars and watched the airplane turn again and taxi toward him. Now the sun was reflecting off the windshield of the Cessna, and Todd couldn't make out either of the people inside. He stepped back behind a corner of the corrugated metal building next to him and waited for the airplane to pass him, when he could get a better view of its occupants.

Then, from his position at the corner of the hangar opposite, he saw the door across from him go up. Apparently, the owner used a garage-door remote control to operate the big bifold door. The airplane slowed, and he caught sight of a wingtip as it turned away from him. Now he could look around the corner and see the whole airplane, but as it entered its hangar, the engine died, the airplane came to a stop, and the bifold door came rattling down. He had seen nothing of the occupants.

That was smoothly done, Todd thought. The owner could have stopped, fussed with his airplane, then affixed a tow bar and pushed it backward into the hangar, but instead, he had simply driven it inside. Of course, when he departed the hangar again he would have to push the airplane out, but Todd had no way of knowing when that would be.

There was probably a car inside the hangar, too, so the owner could drive, instead of fly, away. Todd walked from his hiding place toward the hangar, then walked around to the rear corner, looking for a window or an opening that would allow him to see inside, but the place was sealed.

He stepped out from the hangar, and he had to admire the way it was built. There was a bifold door at the rear, as well as in front: the owner could get into his airplane, start the engine, then depart through the rear door, again without exposing himself to people on the ground.

As Todd stood there, a light went on over his head. There was a security spotlight at each corner, and as he looked up, he saw a window on a second story.

He couldn't get far enough away to see who was inside without bumping into another hangar. Todd walked back to the front of the building and looked toward where his Bonanza was parked. The fuel truck was just pulling away from it.

If Teddy Fay was upstairs, Todd hoped he didn't have surveillance cameras, as well as security lighting. He started back toward the FBO to pay his bill and fly back to Manassas.

Upstairs, Teddy was staring at a flat-screen TV, which had been divided into four parts, each assigned to an outside camera.

"What is it?" Lauren asked, walking up behind him and looking at the screens.

"There was a man outside," Teddy said, "but he's gone now."

"There are all sorts of people around here," Lauren said, "especially at this hour on a Sunday."

"You're right," Teddy said, returning the screen to one large one, with CNN on it. "I won't worry about it." He went to his reclining chair to watch the news. "What's for dinner?"

48

Dino sat in the living room of the suite and pored over a list of names of White House women, and their assignments and locations, that Tim Coleman, Will Lee's chief of staff, had faxed over from the White House.

"Who did we miss?" Stone asked.

"Everybody, apparently. There are a couple hundred names on this list."

"Is there anybody, anybody at all who seems likely?"

"Not to me there isn't," Dino replied. He handed the list to Stone. "You take a look at it."

"Of course, Charlotte Kirby didn't look likely to us, until we interviewed her."

"She didn't seem likely until she was dead," Dino reminded him.

"I don't have a clue where to start," Stone said.

"Neither do I."

"You know, if the March Hare hadn't

killed Charlotte Kirby, we'd be happily back in New York, and the Lees would have put this whole thing out of their minds."

"Yeah, and the March Hare would be safe. Charlotte was a murder too far."

"Why was Charlotte a danger to her?" Stone asked.

"Because she was talking to us," Dino said.

"Yes, but she was through talking to us. The newspaper articles put an end to that. She would never have spoken to us again."

"I guess the March Hare didn't know that. The same was true of Milly Hart and Mrs. Brandon. They had told us everything they knew, too, but still Ms. Hare felt she had to kill them."

Stone put down the list of White House women. "So she didn't know enough about our investigation to see that we were getting nowhere."

"Either that, or she just likes killing other women."

"Dino, can you remember a case of a woman who was a serial killer killing other women?"

Dino thought about it. "Now that you mention it, no. Men who are serial killers kill mostly women, and women serial killers always seem to kill men."

"Can you remember a case where a serial killer, male or female, killed this many people for this reason — the elimination of witnesses?"

"Well," Dino said, "maybe that's happened with the Mafia at some point in the past. They sometimes had a tendency to wipe out a list of people they considered threats."

"But these people weren't threats to the March Hare."

"She didn't know that," Dino pointed out. "She just assumed they were."

"And she didn't linger at the scenes. She hit these women in the head — or, in Charlotte's case, shot her — and got out of there, not leaving any trace evidence. Could she be a cop?"

"Stone, everybody in the United States knows how crime-scene evidence is collected and analyzed — you don't have to be a cop anymore. There are three or four very popular TV shows every week that explain it in detail."

"Okay, so it didn't have to be a cop. But she knew which women we were talking to."

"It's Washington, remember? Everybody in town seemed to know who we were talking to."

"There's one possibility we haven't discussed," Stone said.

"Tell me, *please.*"

"Suppose Charlotte's death really was a suicide, not a murder."

"Well, that's a very attractive notion," Dino said, "since it would confirm everything we told the president and the first lady the other night. But how do you explain the lack of prints on the magazine and the ammo in it?"

"Look, we know the March Hare is a very careful killer. Assume for a moment that Charlotte was the March Hare. She may have prepared the gun for use in a future killing, thus wiping the magazine and the ammo free of prints."

Dino looked hopeful. "Now *that,* I like. It makes perfect sense, and it has the wonderful added advantage of making us look right the first time."

"So why am I not calling the president right now and explaining that Charlotte Kirby committed suicide?"

The phone rang, and Stone picked it up. "Hello?"

"Hi, it's Holly."

"Good morning."

"I've had a thought," Holly said.

"Shoot. We're about all out of thoughts."

"What if Charlotte Kirby really did commit suicide? Maybe she just wiped her prints off the magazine and the bullets out of an excess of caution."

Stone laughed.

"What's funny?"

"Great minds think alike," Stone said. "Dino and I were just discussing the same idea."

"You were not!"

"I promise you, we were."

"You just like the idea because it makes you and Dino look better."

"I can't deny that benefit," Stone said, "but you had the idea independently, and you aren't trying to make us look better, are you?"

"Well, since I brought you into this, it makes me look better, too."

"Tell you what," Stone said. "You go see the director right now and tell her about our mutual theory. If she buys it, we're out of here."

"She's out of the office today," Holly said. "Maybe tomorrow, too."

"Where is she?"

"She goes places unannounced all the time, and she doesn't share that information with me."

"Should I call the president and tell him?"

Holly thought for a moment. "No, it's better if we go through Kate. That way, if she likes it, we'll have her on our side, and she can take it to the president."

"I like the idea of her taking it to the president. I'd just as soon not see him for a while, myself."

"You don't sound entirely convinced of our theory," Holly said.

"I'm afraid to be entirely convinced of anything," Stone said. "Once bitten, you know."

"I know. Well, we can wait until Kate is back in the office, or you can go to the president now. What's your choice?"

"What's your advice?"

"I'd wait for Kate. I'd like to have her on our side."

"I can't argue with that," Stone said. "Dinner tonight?"

"What else have I got to do?" Holly said. "I can shake loose here by seven."

"See you then." Stone hung up and explained to Dino.

"Okay," Dino said, standing up and stretching. "I'm going to the Smithsonian."

"What part of the Smithsonian? It's a big place."

"I'll go to the part with all the airplanes, if you'll go with me."

"You're on," Stone said.

49

Stone and Dino stood under a highly polished DC-3, with Eastern Airlines markings, suspended from the ceiling of the museum. "Isn't that gorgeous?" Stone asked.

"It sure is," Dino said. "I took my first airplane ride in one of those, from the old La Guardia Marine Air Terminal to Boston."

"That airframe could really take it. Some of them did more than a hundred thousand hours."

Dino tapped Stone's elbow. "Look at that," he said.

Stone followed Dino's gaze to where a woman had set down a large handbag and was rummaging through it for something. This went on and on, with objects being removed from the bag, until she finally came up with a tiny camera. She took a photo of the DC-3, then tossed the camera back into her bag, along with all the things she had removed.

"Can you believe it?" Dino asked. "Why do they carry all that stuff around? Shelley has one just as bad."

"Holly, bless her heart, takes a more male attitude," Stone said. "She actually has pockets in some of her clothes."

They moved on to another exhibit.

They were standing in front of the first American spacecraft when Stone's cell phone buzzed.

"Hello?"

"Stone, it's Kerry Smith, at the FBI."

"Hello, Kerry."

"I wonder if you and Dino could come and see me tomorrow morning? I'd like an update on your investigation, if you have the time."

"Actually, Kerry, tomorrow morning might be an ideal time to brief you. What time?"

"Eleven o'clock, in my office?"

"See you then." Stone hung up and turned to Dino. "Kerry Smith wants a briefing on our investigation tomorrow at eleven."

"Sounds like a good time to pull the rip cord and bail out of this mess," Dino said.

"And maybe by that time Holly will have been able to brief Kate Lee, and she, the president."

"I like it," Dino said. "We can burn all our bridges at once."

"Yeah, then we can beat it out of town before another body turns up."

"I'm not going to be responsible for explaining any more corpses after that," Dino said.

Stone's phone went off again. "Hello?"

"It's Holly. I went back to the cell phone locator program, and Fair Sutherlin's phone is alive again and on the move."

"Where is it?"

"Let's see: it's moving right past the Smithsonian Institution right now. Seems to be stuck in traffic outside the Air and Space wing."

"Holy shit! That's where we are!" Stone grabbed Dino's arm and ran for the door. "Come on!"

Dino was trying to keep up with the longer-legged Stone. "What the fuck is going on?"

"It's Fair's cell phone!" They hit the front door running, attracting the notice of a uniformed security guard. Stone stood on the front steps of the museum, looking up and down the street.

"Will you please tell me what you're doing?" Dino asked plaintively. "Maybe I can help."

"Fair Sutherlin's cell phone has come to life, and it's right here in front of us!" Stone put his phone to his ear. "Are you still there, Holly?"

"Yes, what do you see?"

"A bunch of traffic, stopped by a traffic cop. There's a fender bender down the street. What am I supposed to look for?"

"How should I know? It could be in one of those cars. It could be in somebody's pocket. It could be in the gutter!"

The cop was waving traffic on, now, and the line began to move. "What do you see, Dino?"

"Traffic and pedestrians, what else?"

"Fair's cell phone is here somewhere."

"Stone?"

"Yes, I'm here."

"The phone is moving again and picking up speed."

"We're talking about fifty cars, at least," Stone said. "There's nothing we can do about it."

"Are there any unusual vehicles?"

"No, there are half a dozen of those plain vanilla government sedans with government seals you see all over town. There's a moving van, a tow truck, one Rolls-Royce, and a zillion assorted cars."

"Shit," Holly said. "Where is your car?"

"Illegally parked down the street. Don't worry, you'll get the ticket."

"Run for it. I'll keep an eye on where it's headed and direct you."

"I'll call you back when we're on the move." He ended the call. "Come on, Dino, we're going to chase that phone." The two of them sprinted a block and a half down the avenue, got into the car, and got it started. Stone called Holly's cell number.

"I'm here. Go straight ahead for four blocks and turn right on Fourteenth Street. It's about ten blocks ahead of you."

"There's a lot of traffic," Stone said.

"You've got flashers on that car," she said, "use them, but don't use the siren."

"Dino, find the switch for the flashers!"

Dino found the switch. "Have we got a siren?" He found the switch, and the noise began.

"Damn it, Stone," Holly yelled, "I told you not to use the siren!"

"What? I can't hear you! Dino, turn off the damned thing!"

Dino found the switch again, and now Stone could hear Holly screaming.

"You don't have to yell, now," he yelled. "It's off."

"All right. When you get to Pennsylvania Avenue, turn right. The White House will be to your left."

Stone muscled the car in and out of lanes and began to make headway. "I'm turning right on Pennsylvania!"

"Tell Dino to call out the landmark buildings as you pass them, that way I'll know whether you're catching up," Holly said.

"Dino, call out the names of buildings as you see them!"

"Okay, we've got the IRS on the right," Dino said. "Hoover Building coming up, now the National Archives, now the Federal Trade Commission. I can see the Capitol up ahead."

"Hold it!" Holly shouted. "I've lost it."

"Where?" Stone asked.

"I don't know — somewhere on Pennsylvania Avenue. It just vanished."

"I'm pulling over and waiting until you locate it again," Stone said, then did so. He sat for fifteen minutes.

"Nope, it's gone," Holly said. "Nice try, though."

"Gee, thanks," Stone said.

"Well," Dino said, "that's gotta be our last clue. The battery is going to run down eventually."

Stone struck the steering wheel with his

open hand. “Shit! We’re not going to be able to claim the March Hare is dead while that cell phone is out there!”

50

Stone, Dino, Holly, and Shelley dined at Clyde's, in Georgetown, just to get out of the hotel suite. As they entered, Stone whispered to Holly, "Don't tell Shelley about Fair's cell phone. We're meeting with Kerry Smith tomorrow morning, and we may not want to introduce that information into the mix."

"I'm invited, too," Holly replied, "and don't worry, I don't want to bring it up either."

Everybody ordered a steak, and Stone ordered a bottle of a good California Cabernet. The mood was less festive than it usually was.

A camera flash went off, temporarily blinding everyone.

"Who the hell was that?" Dino demanded.

"I can't even see you," Shelley replied, "let alone whoever pulled that trigger."

"My vision is coming back," Holly said,

"and I don't see anyone with a camera, or even anybody looking at us."

"I didn't know Washington had paparazzi," Dino said.

"Forget that," Holly said. "Kate Lee got back this afternoon, and we had the conversation."

"What conversation?" Shelley asked.

"The one where I told her that the investigation is over, that we all think Charlotte Kirby is the March Hare and that she killed herself." She explained their thoughts about the lack of fingerprints on the magazine and ammo.

"Is that what you're telling Kerry tomorrow morning?"

"Yep."

"I'm on board with that. I'm as sick as you are of this whole business."

"Unanimity can't hurt," Stone said. "You think Kerry will back us?"

"Stone, if you believe it, and if I believe it, we can make him believe it, too."

"That's fine, unless Kerry suddenly comes up with some evidence we don't know about."

"Kerry has been up to his ears with our new budget since you got here," Shelley said. "He hasn't had time to deal with anything else."

"Good. My son is opening his first play at Yale this weekend, and I want to be there."

"I want to be there, too," Dino said, "since my boy is the producer. I'm counting on him to make a big success so he can take care of me in my old age."

"I want Kerry to issue a press release," Holly said, "saying that the investigation is now closed. We need that."

"That's problematical," Shelley said. "Kerry is a cautious man. He's not going to want to nail himself to that kind of statement. I think it's better if the White House issues the announcement."

"I don't think the president is the person to issue a statement about a criminal investigation," Holly said, "and I don't think the first lady will think so, either."

"The attorney general, then," Shelley said.

"He's not involved in this," Holly pointed out. "This should be done at Kerry's level. I'm not suggesting that the director of the FBI put his imprimatur on it."

"You can try, but I'm beginning to get the feeling that I'm going to be the one to carry the water on this."

"Maybe an assistant director is good enough," Holly said, "but Kerry is worth a shot."

■ ■ ■ ■

The following morning, Stone and Dino drove over to the Hoover Building, parked in the basement garage, and took the elevator up to the executive floor, where Kerry Smith received them. Holly and Shelley were already there.

After offering them coffee, Kerry tossed a copy of the *Washington Times* onto the coffee table, open to an inside page. "You all look as if you're enjoying yourselves," he said.

Stone picked up the paper and saw the photograph taken of them the previous evening. They were all named, except Holly, who had a menu in the way, and she was called "an unidentified woman."

Stone passed the paper around.

"Why couldn't I be the 'unidentified woman'?" Shelley asked.

"We were just having dinner, Kerry," Stone said. "We can't worry about some gossip guy with a camera."

"Of course not," Kerry replied. "Okay, tell me where you are and where you're going with your investigation."

"Where we are is at the end," Stone said. "Where we're going is back to New York."

"Have you told the president this?"
"We thought we'd let the first lady do that."
"She told him last night," Holly said. "He apparently took it well."
"And who's going to explain all this to the media?" Kerry asked.
"That would be you," Holly said.
"Gee, thanks."
"It shouldn't come from the director, nor from someone any lower than you."
"Just what would you like me to say?"
"Send a fax to the AP and Reuters, and to the big papers, if you want to, saying that an investigation has determined that the probable murderer was Charlotte Kirby, who then took her own life."
"The 'probable' murderer?"
"All right, the likely murderer. Or just the murderer. You shouldn't sound uncertain." She explained about the absence of fingerprints on the gun's magazine and the ammunition.
"I guess that's a decent theory," Kerry said. "Where is the Arlington PD in all this?"
"I took it away from them as soon as I heard about it," Shelley said, "on the grounds that Kirby was a federal employee. Dave King and his people own the case."

"Have Dave King write a memo to you, recommending that the case be concluded, and copy me."

"I'll get it done this morning," Shelley replied.

"I'm going to have to run this by the director."

"Of course, Kerry, by all means," Holly said. "Nobody's trying to hang you out to dry. We've all bought into this."

"Is that true?" Kerry asked, looking at the group.

Everybody nodded.

"Okay. You all have a second cup of coffee while I take this down the hall to the director." He put on his coat and left the office.

"I thought that went well," Holly said.

"It went well only if the director buys it," Shelley said.

They chatted desultorily for the minutes before Kerry re-turned.

"All right," he said, "the director is on board. As soon as I get Dave King's memo and Shelley's written recommendation, we'll get it on the wire services, probably around five. Everybody, and that includes all of you, will be unavailable for comment. Clear?"

There was a murmur of assent, then everybody went their separate ways.

■ ■ ■ ■

Back in the car, Dino drove out onto Pennsylvania Avenue. "I feel relieved," he said.

"I'll feel relieved when we've got wheels up," Stone said. "It'll have to be in the morning. There's a line of thunderstorms between here and New York that I'm not going to fly through, because I don't want to die."

"Once again, we agree," Dino replied. "I don't want to die, either."

51

Stone and Dino got back to the Hay-Adams, and Holly followed close behind. Holly called her office from the bedroom and then made several other calls.

Stone went into the bedroom. "We're ordering lunch. You want something?"

"A club sandwich on rye with mayo and a Diet Coke," Holly said, covering the phone. "Let me know when it comes." She went back to talking on the phone.

As Stone came out of the bedroom, Dino was hanging up the other line. "Shelley's going to join us for a second farewell dinner. She insisted."

"Okay with me," Stone said, "but I know this is because you just want to get laid one more time before we fly out of here."

"There's that, too," Dino said.

Lunch arrived, and Stone went to get Holly, who was still on the phone.

"Just keep a lid on the sandwich," she

said, covering the receiver again. "I'll be there when I can."

Stone went back to the room service table and watched as the waiter served his pasta. He was ravenously hungry, he discovered.

Dino took a bite out of his bacon cheeseburger, then switched on the TV to find the Yankees game.

While Dino watched in silence, Stone ran over the whole of their stay there, looking for some glitch, some loophole they hadn't covered. Apart from the missing cell phone, he could think of nothing.

Holly finally came out of the bedroom, sat down, and uncovered her sandwich. "I'm sorry about that," she said. "I've been on a conference call with Tim Coleman at the White House and Kerry Smith. They finally hammered out a press release that we all agreed on. I represented the first lady in the argument."

"Was it all that tough?" Stone asked.

"To get the White House, the CIA, and the FBI to agree on language? It doesn't get any tougher than that."

"Are you happy with what they came up with?"

"It'll work, I think. The trick was to issue a statement that wouldn't set off a wildfire of press questions. Everybody just wants this thing to die, now."

"How about the D.C. and Arlington PDs?" Dino asked. "Were they consulted?"

"Are you kidding? I wasn't about to open up that can of worms, and Kerry wasn't either. He'll call them and make sure they either decline comment or give bland answers, not disagreeing with the statement, if the media persist in going to them."

"God," Dino said, "this whole business has made me appreciate how simple being an NYPD lieutenant is. Detect crime, solve crime, hand over to DA. That's so nice, compared to what you have to go through in this town."

"I agree entirely," Holly said. "I hate getting involved with police departments. We're not supposed to dabble in domestic affairs, and it always makes me nervous when I have to talk to them, and especially ask them for favors."

They finished lunch and watched the game for the remainder of the afternoon.

Shortly after five o'clock Stone's phone buzzed once on his belt, and a little chime sounded. "E-mail," he said, pulling out the phone. He looked at the message. "It's the statement from the FBI." He read aloud: " 'Shelley Bach, assistant director of criminal investigation of the Federal Bureau of Investigation, announced today that the investigation into the deaths of Mr. and Mrs. Brixton Kendrick and the subsequent deaths of four women — Milly Hart, Muffy Brandon, White House Deputy Chief of Staff Fair Sutherlin, and staffer Charlotte Kirby — has been concluded. Mr. Kendrick's death has been confirmed as a suicide, as has the death of Ms. Kirby. It has also been concluded that the murders of the other four women were committed by Charlotte Kirby, before she took her own life.

" 'White House Chief of Staff Tim Coleman said that the White House concurs with the results of the investigation and will have nothing further to say on the subject. Assistant Director Bach said, "Our investigation is closed, and the FBI will have no further comment." ' "

"So they hung it on Charlotte, after all," Holly said.

It was nearly eight o'clock when Shelley bustled into the suite. "God in Heaven," she said, dropping her large handbag on the desk, "my cell phone hasn't stopped since the release hit." As if to confirm this, a sound like an old-fashioned telephone was emitted from the bag. Shelley, rummaging inside, came up with the phone and switched it off. "Now," she said, "the media can go straight to voice mail!"

Dino poured a scotch and handed it to her. "I think you need this."

"Thank you, I certainly do," she said, downing half of the brown whiskey in one gulp.

"Let me give you the other half of that," Dino said, taking her glass from her. He replenished it, then returned it to her fist.

She downed half of that, too.

"Easy," Stone said. "We don't want to have to send you home in an ambulance."

"It's the only thing that will simultaneously stop the adrenaline and restore the soul," she said. "I've been fielding phone calls for three hours, always saying 'no comment' in one way or another. These people are relentless."

"Let's get some food into you," Stone said, handing out menus.

"First, I have to spend ten minutes in the ladies'," Shelley said, "if you will excuse me." She got up and left the room, taking the remainder of her scotch with her.

"That is one frazzled girl," Holly said. "But by morning, it will be over, and her life will return to normal." Holly's cell phone began to ring.

"And when will your life return to normal?" Stone asked.

Holly checked the calling number. "It's my office," she said. "I have to take this." She pressed a button. "Hello?" She listened for a moment. "Where is it?" She listened again. "Hang on." She covered the receiver with her hand. "It's our Tech Services," she said. "They've got another hit on Fair Sutherlin's cell phone."

"Oh, no," Dino said, putting his face in his hands.

"Where is it?" Stone asked wearily.

Holly turned back to her phone. "Where? At Sixteenth and H Streets?"

"That sounds familiar," Stone said.

"It's the Hay-Adams Hotel."

Stone stared at her. *"Here?"*

Holly went back to her phone. "Call the number," she said, then waited.

Stone and Dino waited, too.

Then, faintly, from across the room, came the tinny, electronic sound of a band playing "The Stars and Stripes Forever," by John Philip Sousa.

The three of them turned and stared at Shelley Bach's handbag.

52

Todd Bacon sat at his desk, working. He continued until eight P.M., when most of the staff in his department had left the building. Todd tidied his desk, locked his case files in his safe, then took a walk around Technical Services. The only people working were on computers, seemingly tracking a cell phone location.

Todd walked to the weapons room, responsibility for the securing of which was his, as the senior officer present. He went into the vault and picked up an ordinary-looking briefcase. He set it on the steel table in the middle of the room and opened it, checked the contents carefully, then he took two loaded magazines from a shelf, put them into the briefcase, closed the door behind him, and turned the combination lock.

He switched off the overhead lights, put on his jacket, and left the department, then the building. He drove out of the Agency grounds and headed for the southeastern side of the District of Columbia, setting Clinton Field into the navigator, since he had never driven there. It would take him the better part of an hour to arrive and get set.

Teddy Fay and Lauren Cade began working in their kitchen in the hangar apartment at Clinton Field. Teddy put some oil and butter into a large pan with a little salt, then added twelve ounces of Arborio rice. He stirred the rice until it was golden, then began adding chicken stock, while Lauren browned a pound of Italian sweet sausages.

Teddy stirred continuously for twenty-five minutes while adding stock to the rice, as Lauren sliced the sausages into bite-sized chunks. After the rice had absorbed the carton of stock and was thick, Teddy added half a carton of crème fraîche and half a cup of grated *Parmigiano Italiano,* while continuing to stir, then he added some green peas that he had cooked earlier and folded them into the dish.

Lauren had set the table and opened a bottle of Amarone, a full-bodied Italian wine. She brought the plates to Teddy, and he heaped the risotto onto them.

■ ■ ■ ■

Todd Bacon parked across the street from Clinton Field, took the briefcase, and climbed over a fence around a water tank nearby. He judged the distance to the hangar's lighted upstairs windows as about forty yards. He climbed the ladder to the top of the tank, about sixty feet high, then he set down the briefcase and opened it, exposing an unassembled Czech-made sniper rifle from the Cold War era.

He assembled the weapon in the dim light as he had practiced in his office the day before, then he screwed the silencer and telescopic sight into place and shoved a magazine into the lightweight rifle.

He sighted the weapon on the upstairs window of the hangar, and he could plainly see a man and a woman working at a stove. He swung the rifle to his right, took aim at a spot at the corner of another hangar, then he racked the action of the rifle and squeezed off a round. He could see it strike exactly where he had aimed.

He swung the rifle back to the kitchen window and watched the woman carry two plates to a table and open a bottle of wine. She sat, facing the window, and Teddy pulled out a chair next to her. Teddy bent over and kissed her on the ear, then he lifted her chin and kissed her on the lips.

Todd aimed at the back of Teddy's head and squeezed off the round.

"I love you," Teddy whispered into Lauren's ear, then he put a finger under her chin and tilted her head. He kissed her lovingly, then started to sit down. As he did so, there were the simultaneous sounds of glass breaking and a thud near him, as a chunk of Lauren's forehead blew away and blood and brain matter spattered the wall behind her. Teddy knew, instantly, that she was dead, and he dove for the floor, as another bullet struck a plate of risotto and scattered it.

More shots came through the metal side of the hangar, as the shooter tried to find him on the floor, but Teddy had quickly crawled away from the window. He heard someone shout from across the street.

"Shit!" Todd yelled at the top of his lungs. Todd quickly disassembled the rifle, closed the briefcase, clenched the handle in his teeth, and jumped for the ladder, clamping it between his feet and sliding down it to the ground in seconds. He tossed the brief-case over the fence, then backed off and got a running start at it. He hit the middle of the fence with his left foot, and his momentum carried him up and over it. He grabbed the briefcase and ran for his car.

From the kitchen floor, huddled under the sink, Teddy heard the vehicle drive away. Teddy had no doubt who the shooter had been. He got an army blanket from the bedroom and spread it over Lauren's body, then, brushing away tears and regaining complete control of himself, he went to the computer and logged on to the CIA mainframe. In less than a minute he was into the personnel files, and seconds after that, he had Todd Bacon's home address. Teddy knew exactly where it was, since it was only a quarter-mile or so from his former home.

Teddy went to the bedroom, grabbed his ready bag, then took a roll of duct tape and wrapped it around Lauren's body in the blanket. He lifted her onto his shoulder and took her downstairs to the hangar, where he set her gently down, then removed the passenger door from the airplane and stowed it in the rear seat.

Feeling no time pressure, Teddy went back upstairs, cleaned up the gore in the kitchen, then tidied up. He sat down and ate some of the risotto, since he didn't want to run out of steam later, then he put the rest down the garbage disposal and the dishes into the dishwasher and started it.

He found a bottle of window cleaner and a dishcloth, and he went around the entire apartment, wiping down every surface that either he or Lauren might have touched. He went to his safe and removed his weapons and tools and took them down to the airplane, then he turned off the lights and went down to the hangar.

He found a pair of aircraft jacks that, he reckoned, weighed forty pounds together, and a length of chain. He lifted Lauren's body into the passenger seat and wrapped the chain around her waist, then, using shackles from his tool kit, fastened the jacks to the chain, setting them on the floor of the passenger side. Finally, he fastened the passenger seat belt around Lauren. He stowed his tools in the luggage compartment, then he did a walk-around of the airplane, checked the fuel, got into the pilot's seat, and started the engine.

A moment later, he used the remote control to open the rear bifold door, and he taxied the airplane out of the hangar, down the taxiway to the airfield's single runway. He looked for traffic on final approach, saw none, heard none on the radio, and, without slowing or announcing his intentions on the air, taxied onto the runway and shoved the throttle forward.

He took off and climbed to seven hundred feet and headed for the Potomac River, then he flew down the river to the bay, then turned and headed for open water. He descended to a hundred feet, turned on the autopilot, and set the altitude hold, then he flew a good ten miles offshore. When he had reached that distance, he undid the passenger seat belt, dropped the two jacks overboard, and let them pull Lauren's body out of the airplane and down into the sea. Then he reversed his course and, finally, turned toward Manassas Airport.

Todd Bacon drove erratically away from Clinton Field, panting for breath and sweating profusely, his car weaving along the roadway. He prayed that there was no cop in the neighborhood, for he would surely be stopped for drunk driving.

As he put distance between himself and the airport, his breathing and pulse returned to something like normal, but he reckoned his blood pressure was still high. The feeling of panic was somewhere in his chest, just deep enough to allow him to drive the car normally.

He reached his home in Virginia, a new town house development, and got the car into the garage, where he sat for several minutes, taking deep breaths and trying to calm down. Finally, he dragged himself into the house, got out of his clothes, and fell, naked and exhausted, onto the bed.

Images of Lauren Cade's exploding head still fired in his brain, but gradually they went away, and he fell into a deep sleep.

53

While Stone and Holly stood and stared at Shelley's handbag, Dino walked over to it and began rummaging inside. Finally, exasperated, he took hold of the bag, turned it upside down, and emptied the contents onto the desktop.

Stone and Holly walked over and gazed at the jumbled heap of the bag's contents. Holly poked around with a finger and came up with a lighted cell phone, the source of the music. "This was missing from the scene of Fair Sutherlin's murder, remember?"

"I remember," Stone said, "but look at this." He picked up a second cell phone, then, rummaging through the pile, came up with four others. "One of these is Shelley's," he said, "and I'd be willing to bet a large sum that the others belong to Mimi Kendrick, Milly Hart, Charlotte Kirby, and Muffy Brandon."

"Souvenirs," Dino said. "Serial killers

often take souvenirs from their victims."

"So I made a mistake," Shelley said from the bedroom doorway.

The others turned to look and found her pointing a 9mm semiautomatic handgun at them, FBI combat–style.

"One little mistake," Shelley repeated. She seemed to tighten her grip on the weapon.

"Shelley, are you going to kill us all to cover yourself?" Stone asked. "That won't work. People saw you enter the hotel. You're well known by now to the staff. You can't kill everybody."

Shelley thought about it. "Dino," she said, "I want you to do exactly as I say."

"That depends on what you say, Shelley," Dino replied.

"I want you to pick up my bag and hold it open, and, Stone, I want you to rake everything on the desktop into the bag. And don't either of you try to use a weapon or I will have to kill you all."

Dino shrugged, picked up the bag, and held it open. Stone raked the pile of junk, including all the cell phones, into the bag.

"Now what?" Dino asked.

"Bring it over here and set it on the floor three feet in front of me," Shelley said.

Dino did as she directed.

Shelley, keeping her pistol pointed at

them, picked up her handbag and backed over to the door. She set it down, opened the door, then picked up the bag and backed out of the suite, letting the door slam behind her.

Dino produced his own weapon and started for the door.

"Let her go, Dino," Stone said. "We can't have a gunfight in the hotel." He got out his cell phone, looked up a number in his frequently called list, and pressed it. He waited for a moment. "This is Stone Barrington. I met with Deputy Director Smith this morning. I want to speak to him immediately. This is an extreme emergency. I'll hold while you find him." Stone covered the phone with his hand. "Let's let the FBI deal with this," he said.

"We should call the DCPD, too," Dino reminded him.

"Let Kerry do that. His word will carry more weight."

Dino walked to the terrace door and opened it. Hot D.C. air flooded into the room, as did noise from the traffic below.

"Stone? It's Kerry Smith. What's wrong?"

"Listen to me carefully, Kerry: it's not over. Charlotte Kirby was not the March Hare. The March Hare is Shelley Bach."

There was a brief silence. "Tell me this is a joke."

"It is not a joke. We've just found the cell phones of the five murdered women in Shelley's handbag. She pointed a gun at us, then took her bag and left our suite at the Hay-Adams."

"She's headed down Sixteenth Street," Dino called from the terrace. "Her car is a silver SUV, a BMW, I think."

Stone repeated that information to Kerry Smith. "She's armed and dangerous, Kerry, and we have no idea where she's headed."

"Can you back this up with evidence, Stone?" Kerry asked.

"The evidence is in her handbag," Stone replied, "and Dino Bacchetti, Holly Barker, and I can testify to that."

"How many phones were in the bag?"

"Six, in all. One must have been Shelley's. We called Fair Sutherlin's phone, and Shelley's bag began to ring."

"How about the other four? Can you swear that they belong to the other victims?"

"No, that's just our assumption. You'd do well to capture that bag, as well as Shelley."

"All right, I'll issue the orders immediately. You three stay there. I'm going to send some agents to talk to you."

"We'll be right here," Stone said, and

hung up. He put the phone into its holster, went to the bar, and poured himself a stiff bourbon. "Anybody else?"

"Me," Dino said.

"Me," Holly said.

Stone poured the drinks, and they all sat down.

Dino was the first to speak. "I've been sleeping with a serial murderer since we arrived in this town," he said.

"Do you know," Stone said, "that in all our investigating and checking, we never checked the whereabouts of Shelley at the times of the various murders? Not once?"

"When she got called to go to the White House, after Mrs. Kendrick's murder, she was already at the White House," Dino said.

"It never occurred to me," Holly said. "She was the FBI's lead investigator on all the murders. If she hadn't hung on to those phones, nobody could ever have made even one of the charges stick."

"So, she was just one of Brix Kendrick's conquests," Dino said.

Stone nodded. "She eliminated Mimi from Kendrick's life. That makes sense — she wanted him to herself. Then, when he didn't play that way, she started taking revenge."

"And she was right among us the whole

time," Dino added. "She knew every detail of our investigation from day one."

Holly took a swig of her scotch. "And now I'm going to have to call the first lady and director of my agency and tell her that we got it wrong."

"That we got it wrong twice," Stone said. "At our dinner with the Lees, when we told them Charlotte Kirby was the killer, and, of course, now."

"We're going to look like assholes," Dino said. "Amend that: we *are* assholes."

"You're not going to get an argument from me," Stone said.

Holly said nothing.

Stone got up and started toward the bedroom.

"Where are you going?" Dino said. "The FBI will be here in a minute."

"I'm going to pack," Stone said. "Then I'm going to answer their questions for as long as it takes. Then I'm going to get the hell out of D.C."

Dino got up and started toward his bedroom. "Good idea," he shouted over his shoulder.

"Fellas," Holly called out, "this may take longer than you think."

54

Stone answered the doorbell, and Special Agent Dave King stepped inside and introduced his partner, Special Agent Ann Potter.

"Now," King said, "tell me what the hell is going on here."

"Dave," Stone said, "do you remember that when we visited the crime scene at Fair Sutherlin's apartment, Shelley Bach asked if you had found her cell phone?"

"Yes, I do," King said. "We had not found it."

"That's because it was in Shelley's handbag at that moment. She had taken it on an earlier visit that afternoon, after she murdered Ms. Sutherlin."

"Are you completely nuts?" King asked.

"Listen to me, Dave: Holly had the CIA do a search for the Sutherlin cell phone, and it was at this hotel. She had them call the number, and we heard it go off. It was in Shelley's handbag."

"Shelley was here?"
"She was. She was in the bathroom when the phone rang. We emptied out her bag, and there were six phones in it. We believe one was Shelley's and the others belonged to the five women."
"You don't know that," King said.
"She came out of the bathroom with a gun in her hand, took the bag, and left."
"I don't believe this."
"Holly," Stone said, "can you put traces on the other four cell phones, and on Shelley's, as well?"
"I've got Shelley's number," Dino said.
"I've got Milly Hart's," Stone said. "Don't bother with the Kendrick phone. She's been dead for a year. Can you get the numbers for Brandon and Kirby?"
"Of course," Holly said. "I'll be right back." She went into the bedroom to use the phone.
King spoke again. "You're telling me that an assistant director of the FBI is a serial killer?"
"That's exactly what I'm telling you, Dave. Are your people looking for Shelley yet?"
"That's my call, and I'm not convinced," King said.
Stone looked at his watch. "She could

already be out of the District," he said. "How long are you going to wait?"

Holly came back into the room. "My people are on it." She went to Stone's computer and logged on to the CIA mainframe. "Well, well, look at this," she said, pushing back from the laptop so the others could see.

Stone and King walked to the computer and watched.

Holly pointed. "We've got Sutherlin's, Kirby's, and Shelley's phones at the same point, across the river in Arlington, headed south."

"They're all in the same handbag, Dave, and pretty soon Shelley is going to realize that, and she'll get rid of the phones. You need to catch her while they're in her possession."

King stared at the moving display for a moment, then he took out his own phone and made a call. "This is Dave King," he said. "I want every agent in D.C. and northern Virginia looking for Assistant Director Shelley Bach on a charge of murder. She's in a silver BMW SUV, in Arlington right now, headed south. When she's apprehended, it's very important that you confiscate her handbag immediately. Alert local PDs in the area, as well. Call me immediately when she has been apprehended." He looked at Stone. "You better be right about this."

"You better be right about it, too," Stone said, "or she'll be gone."

Holly spoke up. "Uh-oh," she said.

"What?" Stone asked.

"The cell phones are splitting up. Shelley's still moving, but the other two have stopped. She's ditched them." Holly zoomed in and got a street address.

King got back on the phone. "There are at least two cell phones that have been discarded near this address." He recited the street and number. "I want every trash can and dumpster near there searched, and when found, the phones are to be treated as evidence."

They all watched the screen, and a moment later, Shelley's phone disappeared from it.

"Now she's ditched her own phone," Holly said, "or removed the SIM card. Shelley Bach is now wild in the country."

"Oh, shit," Dave King said.

"She's going to ditch her car, too," Stone said, "if she's thinking clearly."

"She is," Holly said. "She's over the panic now — ditching the phones shows us that."

Dino spoke up. "Let's hope she's winging

it," he said, "because if she has a plan, we're fucked."

"What kind of plan?" Dave King asked.

"Does she have a country place?" Dino asked. "Does she own another car?"

King got back on his phone and started issuing orders again.

"She's had time to think about this," Holly said. "If she's really smart, and I think she is, she has a plan. She has a bolt-hole, and maybe another car, too, not registered in her name. Dave, you should find out who her friends are. If I'm wrong about the bolt-hole, she might go to someone for help."

King nodded, still talking on the phone.

It was nearly midnight before Dave King and his partner left the suite. There had been no further sign of Shelley Bach.

Shortly after he left, the phone rang, and Stone picked it up.

"Hello?"

"This is the White House operator," a woman's voice said. "Will you speak to the president?"

"Of course," Stone said. He heard a click.

"Stone?"

"Yes, sir."

"Please put Dino on an extension."

"Yes, sir. Dino, pick up the bedroom

phone. Holly, get the other one. Mr. President, we're all here."

"Good."

"I'm on the phone, too," Kate Lee said.

"I've heard from Kerry Smith what's going on," the president said.

"We've been brought fully up to date," Kate interjected.

"We both want to thank you for sticking with this until it was resolved," the president said. "At least, it will be when Shelley Bach is caught."

"Dino and I jumped to conclusions the last time we all spoke," Stone said, "and I want to apologize for that."

"We've known Shelley Bach for some years," the president said, "and of course we're shocked. The media have already got wind of this, and the press office here is getting calls. I wanted you to know that. I'd appreciate it if you'd refer any questions to Kerry Smith. They're stunned over there, but it's their case now, and they should be seen to be handling it."

"We will refer questions to the FBI with pleasure, Mr. President, and we'll be out of here tomorrow morning."

"Have a good flight back, then, and if you're in Washington again before we're done here, come and have dinner with us."

"We'd like that, Mr. President."

"Good night to you all," the president said.

"Good night," Kate echoed. "And, Holly, come and see me first thing tomorrow morning."

"Yes, ma'am," Holly said, but they had already hung up.

Dino and Holly came into the living room.

"I don't know about you two," Stone said, "but I'm exhausted."

"Then come to bed," Holly said, heading for the bedroom.

"I guess I'm sleeping alone tonight," Dino said.

55

Teddy set down his Cessna at Manassas Airport well after midnight, then taxied to the FBO, which was dark. Everything, including the tower, was closed.

He went to the luggage compartment, got out a case, took the things he needed, then put the case back and locked the compartment. He removed the passenger door from the rear seat and rehung it on the airframe, then locked the airplane.

He went to the FBO door and inspected it for alarm sensors, then he shone a very bright flashlight around the walls, looking for an alarm box. Finding none, he took a set of lockpicks from his pocket and made quick work of opening the door. Inside, he went to the rental car desk and checked the keys hanging there, then chose one.

He unlocked the rear door of the FBO from the inside and stepped into the parking lot, then he unlocked a Toyota Camry, got in, and started it. A moment later he was on his way to an apartment development a fifteen-minute drive from CIA headquarters.

It was easy enough to find, since there was a large sign at the untended gate offering two- and four-bedroom town houses for rent, furnished or unfurnished. He parked two doors down from Todd Bacon's house, slipped plastic booties on over his shoes, and, using his flashlight sparingly, walked between the two nearest houses to what would be backyards when the landscaping was developed. The ground was dry. He checked the two houses as he moved along, looking for signs of alarm systems, but he saw none. Bacon's house would be alarmed only if he had installed the system himself, and he was unlikely to have done that for a rental.

Teddy circumnavigated Bacon's house, figured out where the ground-floor master bedroom was, then decided that the best way in was the front door. He slipped out of his shoes and booties on the lawn next to the front walk and continued in his stocking feet. On the front porch, he stopped and prepared the materials he had brought with him. The moon gave him all the light he needed.

He donned latex gloves and picked the front door lock easily — it was right out of a hardware store — and let himself into the front hall, silently closing the door behind him. He stopped in the entrance hall for a full minute, listening for signs of life in the house. A faint snore came from the direction of the master bedroom, down the hallway. He walked slowly down the hall, the silenced gun held out in front of him, took a quick look through the open bedroom door, then jerked his head back and reviewed what he had seen.

Todd Bacon lay on his back, on the left side of the bed, snoring with each breath. The bedroom was flooded with moonlight. Teddy removed the small plastic hypodermic from his shirt pocket, uncapped it, put the cap into his trousers pocket, then clenched the instrument in his teeth. He walked softly into the bedroom, around the bed, and stopped next to the sleeping man. He took the hypodermic from his mouth, bent over until his lips were near Bacon's ear, then poked the silencer hard against his temple. "Freeze!" he said. "Not a move, not an eyelash."

Bacon's eyes opened, and he did not move. Teddy plunged the short needle of the hypodermic into his carotid artery and pressed the plunger, then pulled it out and set it on the bedside table. This would only take a minute, he knew. When he had been at the CIA, they had tested the drug, first on animals, then on volunteers.

"It's going to feel nice," Teddy said. "You'll feel warm all over, and you'll be able to see and hear, but you won't be able to move or speak. Don't worry, it won't kill you." He pressed his fingers against the artery and felt for the pulse. He could feel its rapidity, then it slowed. It was done.

"You just lie quietly there for a minute," Teddy said. "I'll be ready for you shortly." He left the paralyzed man and went into the bathroom. He switched on the light and looked around, checked the medicine cabinet. Then he saw what he wanted, standing in a drinking glass on top of the sink. He walked to the bathtub, closed the drain, and turned on the water, testing the warmth. He wanted it hot. Then he returned to the bedroom.

Bacon's body was twitching a little as he tried and failed to move. Teddy removed the plastic cap from his pocket, capped the needle, and put the hypodermic into his pocket. Then he pulled back the covers, exposing Bacon's naked body, then took the man's head in his hands and dragged him from the bed onto the floor. He took hold of Bacon's wrists and dragged him into the bathroom, then he muscled the inert form into the bathtub.

"You're going to have a nice hot bath," Teddy said, "then you're going to die."

Bacon's eyes swiveled and looked at him, seeming to open wider. "Lauren never knew what hit her when you fired that shot," Teddy said, "but you're going to know everything." He went to the sink and took the straight razor from the glass on the sink. He had planned to use a kitchen knife, but this was much better. He returned to the bathtub and, in turn, made an incision in each of Bacon's wrists, parallel with the forearm, then he dropped the hands back into the water.

"This is how you commit suicide with a razor," Teddy said. "You don't cut across the wrist, but along it. You bleed a lot more that way. Now, you have a couple of minutes before you lose consciousness. Use it to think about the stupid thing you did. Use it to think about that beautiful young woman whose life you took. Your autopsy will show that your cause of death was suicide by blood loss. They'll never think to do a tox screen, and even if they do, it's very unlikely that they'll detect the drug I gave you. No one will ever know why you died but me, and whoever I choose to tell about it.

"Are you a Christian, Todd? I hope so, because then you'll believe me when I tell you that you will wake up in hell, because you committed the sin of murder."

Teddy sat by the tub for another couple of minutes, periodically checking Bacon's pulse. Finally, his heart stopped. His body appeared to be afloat in a bathtub of tomato soup.

Teddy switched off the bathroom light and went back into the bedroom, scuffing the carpet to remove any sign of the body being dragged across the floor. He let himself out of the house, put on his shoes and booties, and walked back to the Toyota.

Half an hour later, Teddy pulled into the parking lot at Manassas Airport, still wearing his gloves and booties. He locked the Toyota and went inside through the back door, locking it behind him. He hung the car keys on the board at the rental counter, let himself out the front door onto the ramp, and locked the door behind him.

Back in the airplane, he retrieved his Apple AirBook. He had a strong signal from the FBO's wireless network. He logged on to the CIA mainframe and sent a single e-mail, then he put away the computer, started the airplane, taxied to the runway, and took off to the south, not turning on his transponder. He flew low until he was sure he was out of Washington Center's airspace, then he climbed to eight thousand feet, set the autopilot, and entered the code AVL into the GPS. He pressed the direct button on the GPS, then the nav button on the autopilot, and let it fly him toward Asheville Regional Airport, in North Carolina.

Now, flying through the smooth night air, the starry sky above him, the green landscape below, he allowed himself to weep for Lauren Cade, and what he had lost.

56

Holly woke up at six and slipped out of bed, leaving Stone still dead to the world. She showered and put on fresh clothes, stuffed the other things she had left at the hotel during Stone's stay into her bag, then she tiptoed out of the suite and went down to her car.

The drive to Langley went quickly, since rush hour was not in full force, and back in her office she found a pastry in the kitchenette she shared with Lance Cabot, then made some coffee.

She took breakfast to her desk, switched on her computer, and while it booted, she shuffled through the mess in her in-box. She had some catching up to do, she reckoned, and she had to go and see the director at nine.

She had just stuffed a large bite of cheese Danish into her mouth when a message slowly materialized on her screen. This was not an ordinary e-mail, and she wondered who had sent it. She did not wonder for long.

> Last night, your minion Todd Bacon, while trying to murder me, instead killed Lauren Cade, who was your friend. Apparently conscience-stricken, Bacon took his own life in the wee hours of this morning.
>
> I will pay you the compliment of believing that you have honored our arrangement, that the attempt on my life was an act of Bacon's own devising, without reference to you or Cabot, and I will conduct myself accordingly. Should you wish to reach me again, place an ad in the Arts section of the national edition of the New York Times, addressed to Wanderer.
>
> Good luck to you.

Holly attempted to print the message, but when she touched a key, it gradually disintegrated and disappeared from the screen.

Lance looked in, his briefcase still in his hand. "Good morning."

Holly was still staring at the screen and did not respond.

Lance stepped into the room, set down

his briefcase, and took a seat across from her. "What's wrong?" he asked.

"I've just had a communication from Teddy Fay," she replied. "I tried to print it, but it disappeared."

"And what did he have to say for himself?"

"Apparently, Todd Bacon went off the reservation last night and went after Teddy. He didn't get him, but, as a result, Lauren Cade was collateral damage."

"Good God," Lance said, his face darkening. "Is Teddy going on another rampage?"

"No, he said he didn't blame you or me, but I think he killed Todd and made it look like a suicide."

"Thank heaven for small favors. Find out if he was telling the truth." Lance picked up his briefcase and went to his own office.

Holly looked up Todd Bacon's home number and called it. She got an answering machine. She tried his office extension and got voice mail. Maybe he was on his way in. It was nearly nine, so she went to the director's office and was shown in immediately.

"Thank you for coming, Holly," Kate Lee said, motioning her to a chair.

Holly sat down and prepared herself for a rebuke.

"I wanted to tell you that I think your idea

of bringing Stone and Dino down here was exactly the right thing to do."

Holly let out the breath she had been holding.

"Frankly, I had expected them to conclude that Brix murdered his wife before killing himself. I am astonished, of course, to see how this has played out, but I don't want you to think that you are in any way responsible for the events following Stone's and Dino's arrival."

"Thank you, ma'am," Holly replied.

"I am, of course, going to be leaving the Agency next year, when Will's term ends. I will resign."

"I'll be sorry to see you leave," Holly said.

Kate smiled. "You can be sure that Lance is already preparing the ground for a shot at this chair, after I go."

"I wouldn't be surprised," Holly said.

"I don't know if he'll get it. That will be up to a new president, but if he does, I'm sure he'll bring you up here with him. If he doesn't, I want you to know that your personnel file will contain the highest possible personal recommendation from me, and I will make a few phone calls, too."

"That's very kind of you, ma'am, and I appreciate it."

"The president has asked me to tell you

that he is very grateful for your work over the past days, and that you may always use him as a reference, whatever you may decide to do. That goes for me, as well."

"Thank you, Director, and please convey my gratitude to the president," Holly said.

"Okay, get back to work, girl." Kate opened a file on her desk and began to read.

Holly went back to her office, and Lance buzzed her to come into his office. "Where have you been?" he asked.

"The director asked me to come up to see her."

"And?"

"She thanked me for bringing Stone and Dino down from New York."

"That's all?"

"She said nice things about me."

"What about me?"

"She said you've probably already begun to do the groundwork for getting her job when she goes."

Lance chuckled. "She knows me well. I have planted the idea in a few places on Capitol Hill, and with a couple of likely candidates for president. And if I get it, I'll want you with me."

"Thank you, Lance."

"Now, what are we going to do about Todd Bacon?"

"I think we should do nothing," Holly said.

"Don't you want to know if he's dead?"

"Yes, but I'm not going to ask. If he is, he'll be discovered in due course. Nobody in this building doesn't not show up for work unless he's called in. If Todd doesn't show, someone will find out why."

"All right, let that sleeping dog lie," Lance said.

Holly went back to her office, and her phone was ringing. "Hello?"

"It's Stone. We're out of here. Dino and I are flying directly to New Haven for Peter's opening tonight."

"I'd send him a telegram if there were still such a thing," Holly said. "Tell him I said break a leg."

"Will do. What should I do with the car?"

"Leave it at the FBO at Manassas, with the keys under the seat. It will be picked up."

"Thank you for such good company while we've been here," Stone said.

"We both needed that, I think."

"Coming to New York anytime soon?"

"You'll be the first to know."

"Take care, then."

They said good-bye and hung up.

■ ■ ■ ■

Holly was working at her desk just before lunch when her phone rang. "Yes?"

"It's Tank Wheeler, in Tech Services."

"Morning, Tank. What can I do for you?"

"Todd Bacon is dead."

Holly took a long beat before answering. "How?"

"When he didn't come in this morning and didn't call, I sent some people over to his place. They broke in and found him in the bathtub with his wrists slit."

"Did Todd seem suicidal to you?"

"Nope. He seemed to be enjoying his work. He had something on his mind, though — he had been preoccupied for a few days."

"Have you any reason to believe it wasn't a suicide?"

"My people had a look around, but there was no evidence of foul play. One odd thing, though: they found a sniper's rifle in a briefcase in Todd's car that he had checked out of the weapons vault yesterday. I've no idea why."

Holly did not comment on that. "Have you called the local police?"

"I'm about to do that right now. I wanted

to tell you first."

"Play it by the book," she said, "except for the sniper's rifle. You can put that back where it belongs and deal with the written record."

"I have already done so."

"We'll want our own pathologist at the autopsy."

"Of course. We'll track the investigation every step of the way and keep the Agency out of the papers."

"Let me know the results," Holly said. "And thanks, Tank." She hung up and went into Lance's office.

He looked up from his desk. "Heard anything?"

"Tank Wheeler just called. When Todd didn't show up for work, he sent some people out there. They found him in the bathtub, bled out. There was an Agency sniper's rifle in his car."

"I see."

"I told Tank to call the police and go by our playbook for such an event. We'll be represented at the autopsy, and of course we'll see the police report. Tank has returned the rifle to the vault and adjusted the record."

"And the Agency will be kept out of it?"

"Of course."

"I guess I'd better start thinking of a replacement for Todd in Tech Services."

"I might be interested," Holly said.

"Not going to happen," Lance said. "Your future at the Agency will depend on how my plans for me work out," he said. "But don't worry, whatever happens, you're thought of as valuable around here."

"Thank you," Holly said, then went back to her office and put Todd Bacon and Teddy Fay out of her mind.

57

Dino parked the car at the Manassas FBO, and he and Stone carried their luggage to the airplane. While Dino stowed the bags, Stone walked around the airplane and did his preflight inspection. He had already gotten a weather forecast — good all the way — from Flight Services and filed his flight plan.

Then Stone remembered a call he had not made. He checked his notebook for the number and the hospital answered. "Dr. Tom Kendrick," Stone said.

After a short wait, Tom Kendrick came on the line. "Dr. Kendrick."

"Dr. Kendrick, this is Stone Barrington. We met at your parents' house."

"I remember," Kendrick said.

"We've concluded our investigation, and I wanted you to know the results."

"I'd like to hear it," Kendrick replied.

"We have concluded that your father did

not kill your mother. The note he left was misinterpreted."

"I'm relieved to hear that," Kendrick replied, "but who did kill her?"

"She was killed by a woman named Shelley Bach, who was having an affair with your father. We believe that your father took his own life because he felt that his affair with Ms. Bach was the root cause of her death. This will all be in the papers by tomorrow, so you'd better prepare yourself for a lot of phone calls from the media."

"Thank you, I'll try to handle that. And thank you for letting me know the outcome." Kendrick hung up.

Stone got aboard, then buttoned up the airplane, started the engines, and ran through his checklist. Finally, he called ground control for his clearance. The controller read him the clearance, and Stone repeated it.

"That's the first time I've ever seen an airplane cleared across the Washington TFR," he said, referring to central Washington, including the White House. "And at low altitude. You must know somebody."

Stone laughed. "No, just the luck of the draw," he replied, and requested permission to taxi. When they had lifted off, Stone said to Dino, "You're going to be impressed with our routing."

"Yeah, why?"

"I think Holly used her influence with Air Traffic Control to see that we got the scenic route."

Moments later they crossed the Potomac at three thousand feet and saw the Washington Monument and the White House ahead.

"Man, what a view!" Dino said. "I'm going to send Holly some flowers!"

Shortly after they had passed the White House, Stone was told to climb directly to his filed cruising altitude and to fly direct to New Haven. Normally, he would have ascended in stages and been told to fly an airway.

They landed at Tweed Field, New Haven, and Dino's son, Ben, drove out onto the ramp to meet them and unload their luggage.

Dino embraced his son, and Stone shook his hand. "We could have taken a cab," Stone said.

"I'm glad to have a break from the theater," Ben said. "Peter will be embroiled with details until curtain time, since he's the director, but I wasn't needed. I'm only the producer."

He drove them to the building where Peter had bought an apartment that housed himself, Ben, and Peter's girlfriend, and Stone and Dino made themselves comfortable in the guest room, while Ben went back to the theater.

"They've done some more fixing up since we were here last," Dino said.

"Yes, they've got curtains and a nice Oriental rug, now," Stone agreed. They found the makings of sandwiches in the fridge and made lunch.

As the final curtain came down, the audience rose as one, applauding, whistling, and shouting. The cast took multiple curtain calls, then, to shouts of "Author! Author!" Peter joined them for the final bow.

"That was really something," Stone said.

"I hadn't expected it to be so funny," Dino replied. "That was terrific writing."

"It certainly was," Stone said. "They're meeting us at the restaurant."

The opening night party was nearly as much of a triumph as the opening night performance. Stone and Dino were treated with deference by the student crowd, but stayed out of the way and let Peter and Ben have their moment of glory.

Finally, Peter joined them at their table.

"It was brilliant, Peter," Stone said.

Dino praised him, as well.

"I've got some news," Peter said. "There was someone from the Shubert Organization in New York in the audience, and it looks like we're going to get an offer to open our play in one of their theaters after Christmas."

"Will you direct?" Stone asked.

"I doubt it," Peter replied. "They'll recast it with New York actors and get a pro to direct. We're just a bunch of students, after all."

"Some bunch of students!" Stone said. "Every one of them was perfection."

"They were, weren't they?" Peter said. "I'll get you guys another drink, and then I have to circulate some more." He left, found a waiter, then blended into the crowd again.

"You know," Stone said to Dino, "I much prefer seeing that play to seeing Peter quarterback Yale to a victory over Harvard."

"I know how you feel," Dino said, "and this way, he doesn't get a concussion."

58

Shelley Bach rinsed under the shower, then got into a robe and toweled her hair. She checked the mirror and approved of what she saw. The new auburn color worked very well for her, or would soon.

She dried her hair and dressed, then went to the basement of the apartment building in Arlington and got into the Honda Civic she had bought earlier, under her new name, using ID she had manufactured using FBI equipment. She drove a couple of blocks down the street, parked at a strip mall, and went into a shop.

"I'm Carly Shaker," she said to the receptionist. "I have an appointment."

"Right this way, Ms. Shaker," the young woman said. She showed her down the hall to a curtained booth and handed her a paper robe. "Undress and put this on, and she will be with you in a moment."

Carly did as she was told, and had a seat.

Another woman, who appeared to be in her mid-thirties, came into the booth and checked a clipboard. "Let's see," she said, "you're getting the full-body airbrush, is that right?"

"That's correct," Carly said. She got up and pointed at a color chart on the wall. "And I think this shade would be good for me. What do you think?"

"Very good," the woman said. "Not too dark, just a lovely shade that will go perfectly with your hair. Now, if you'll take off your robe and stand on the little pedestal, we'll get to work."

An hour later, Carly stood naked before a full-length mirror and stared at her new complexion. Her formerly blond whiteness had been darkened to a nearly Mediterranean shade that blended perfectly with her new hair color. It would last for two weeks, then she would have it touched up.

She got dressed, paid her bill, and drove back to her apartment building, a new woman. Back in her apartment she felt a pang of regret. She took the new, anonymous cell phone she had bought at a Radio Shack, looked up a number, and tapped it in. The phone went directly to voice mail, and she left a message.

That would have to do, for now. Later, who knew?

59

Stone set down the airplane lightly after flying the ILS 19 approach into Teterboro Airport, and was given permission to taxi to Jet Aviation. He was directed to a parking place a few yards from the terminal, and he opened the luggage compartment so that a lineman could unload their luggage onto a cart.

Stone checked the oil in both engines, then opened the rear luggage compartment, disconnected the battery, and handed another lineman the engine plugs and pitot tube covers, to be installed. They followed their luggage into the terminal, then out the front door, where Stone's secretary, Joan, was waiting in Stone's car.

Traffic was light going into the city, and they dropped Dino off at his apartment building, then headed for Turtle Bay, and Stone's house.

■ ■ ■ ■

Dino let himself into his apartment and took his bags into the bedroom, where he unpacked and put everything away, then he went into his study. There was a large stack of mail, mostly bills and junk, on his desk, and he sat down and began sorting and opening it.

Then he noticed that the light on his answering machine was blinking, and he pushed the button to get his messages.

"Hello, Dino," a familiar female voice said. "I've been thinking about you, and I couldn't resist calling."

"Jesus," Dino muttered to himself, then checked the caller ID. "Number Blocked," it read.

"I wanted you to know that I'm all right," she continued. "I had feared something like this might happen, so I made some preparations in advance. I'm in a new place, now, with a new life. Eventually, though, I might get to New York. If I do, would you like to hear from me? Think about that, and I'll call again sometime. In the meantime, I'll think about you in bed, and that little thing you do so nicely. Bye-bye."

Dino hung up and thought for a moment,

then he called Stone's office number.

"Woodman and Weld," Joan said.

"Joan, it's Dino. Let me speak to him."

"Hang, Dino." She put him on hold.

"Hey, Dino," Stone said. "Miss me already?"

"Oh, terribly," Dino said.

"Dinner at Elaine's, eight-thirty?"

"You're on, but I've got news. Guess who left a message on my answering machine?"

Dunn Public Library

ABOUT THE AUTHOR

Stuart Woods is the author of over forty-five novels, including the *New York Times*–bestselling Stone Barrington and Holly Barker series. An avid sailor and pilot, he lives in New York City, Florida, and Maine.

The employees of Thorndike Press hope you have enjoyed this Large Print book. All our Thorndike, Wheeler, and Kennebec Large Print titles are designed for easy reading, and all our books are made to last. Other Thorndike Press Large Print books are available at your library, through selected bookstores, or directly from us.

For information about titles, please call:
(800) 223-1244

or visit our Web site at:
http://gale.cengage.com/thorndike

To share your comments, please write:

Publisher
Thorndike Press
10 Water St., Suite 310
Waterville, ME 04901

DUNN LIBRARY

2016-09-06 12:45

EILEEN HICKS

You have the following items:

---

1. D.C. dead
   Barcode: 33436001409918 Due:
   09/27/2016 11:59 PM

HARNETT COUNTY PUBLIC
LIBRARY
Dunn Library
910-892-2899

>Loan Receipt<

2016-09-06 12:45

Dunn Public Library

Dunn Public Library
110 E. Divine St.
Dunn, NC 28334
892-2899